Suffer Little Children

Alice Maxwell is 82 years old, widowed, crippled with arthritis, game, and clinging desperately to the house in a condemned terrace which has been her home for all her married life.

The high spot of her day is when the local children visit her: five of them, ranging in age from eight to fifteen, latchkey kids of those otherwise deprived emotionally, who are only too ready to batten on Alice and her meagre pension when they want the extras in life which they believe are theirs by right. To Alice they represent company, affection, and when her nights become nights of terror because of sinister sounds in the empty rooms overhead, it never occurs to her that these can have any connection with her daytime visitors. They're only children, after all.

What Alice does not realize is that the children are far advanced on the path of delinquency and are already into organized theft. They stash their loot in her condemned terrace, and they aren't going to see themselves betrayed by an old woman they despise. Despite the well-meant interest of social workers and a kindly taxi-driver, Alice's nights of terror are soon equalled and even surpassed by her days . . .

Sheila Johnson's first novel, written in a white heat of anger, is a shocker. Unsparing in its honesty, mesmeric in its hold upon the reader, it highlights social evils most of us prefer not to be aware of, while exposing us to the consequences of our indifference.

SHEILA JOHNSON

Suffer Little Children

COLLINS, ST JAMES'S PLACE, LONDON

William Collins Sons & Co. Ltd
London · Glasgow · Sydney · Auckland
Toronto · Johannesburg

First published 1981
© Sheila Johnson 1981

British Library Cataloguing in Publication Data

Johnson, Sheila
    Suffer little children. — (Crime Club)
    I. Title
    823'.914 [F]

    ISBN 0-00-231796-6

Photoset in Compugraphic Baskerville
Printed in Great Britain by
T. J. Press (Padstow) Ltd

CHAPTER 1

It was cold, bitterly cold. The winter's draughts, sneaking in around the warped door and window-frames, rising in dirt-streaked lines from beneath the loose skirting-boards, held a sharp edge of ice. But it wasn't merely the bleak November chill that had turned her age-thinned blood to a flesh-shrinking trickle; it was fear.

A helpless, mind-robbing, quivering fear. For the footsteps had started again.

No ordinary footsteps, these, to fall with a steady measured tread that would, however stealthy, at least betray something human in their origin. No, these were just the odd heavy step, out of nowhere. Going nowhere, falling at random to set the boards topping the ceiling above her head creaking in protest.

Stifling a whimper of terror, the old lady clutched at the quilt. With fingers convulsively hooked into talons she clawed at it; drawing it up to her chin and rolling herself into a ball she huddled beneath its padded protection, scarcely daring to breath. Silence beat down on her. Waiting it seemed, like soft wings hovering in the cold, cold darkness, frightening her now almost as much as the footsteps had done. Her faded blue eyes were fixed on the ceiling, probing among the inky shadows in the cracked and crumbling plaster as though she might glimpse whatever was lurking above through some chink in its surface.

Time passed, crawled away, and still she cowered under the bedclothes. She was sweating now in spite of the room's chill but was yet reluctant to surrender her grip on the stifling quilt. The battered alarm clock ticked away a further half-hour before she was able to tear her gaze from its terrified vigil. Slowly she slid her eyes down past the blown cabbage-roses adorning the walls, over the massive, ornately carved tallboy, and round to the clock's familiar face.

Five minutes to midnight. It was much later than the last time, she noted. The footsteps had started well before ten on that occasion, while she had still been up and dressed. Although, crippled as she was, she had been able to do no more than grope her way to the foot of the stairs that led to the overhead rooms and shout, 'Hello! Who is it? What do you want?' up the echoing stairwell. Fear had grown then, as now, from the silence that greeted her quavering enquiry.

There were no neighbours for her to appeal to. No one lived in the half-shells adjoining her home. Indeed, they were only left standing because their removal would have meant taking away her side walls. The walls of Alice's ground-floor rooms formed one side wall of the entry, and since her upstairs rooms ran halfway over the top to meet those of the neighbouring property, most of that house had been left standing when the rest of the row was demolished.

Her house, and all the others built more than a hundred years since in the long, narrow terraces that had once crowded this neighbourhood, had long been scheduled for demolition. One by one the cramped homes had been cleared, their former tenants packed and eager to move on into more spacious accommodation. But she had hung on. Long after the last family had said their goodbyes and moved away, she had remained.

The empty houses were boarded up, ribald slogans and filth bloomed on their walls, weeds began to sprout along the flagstoned pavements. And, as one year gave way to another, Alice burrowed further into her niche, unable to tear herself away from the lifetime of memories stored in these four walls. Undaunted, she had defied all attempts to cajole, persuade, or enforce her removal.

Then the demolition work had commenced all around her. Gangs of men, shepherding home-gobbling machines, had livened each day with their labours until the dust of old bricks hung like a pall over Alice's home.

'That'll soon fetch the stubborn old fool out of the way,' some of the more hardened among the town planners had prophesied with grim satisfaction, but they were to be proved wrong.

More quickly than Alice had ever thought possible, the once overcrowded streets were cleared and razed, until at last only her own house had remained standing. Growing out of the rubble, with the two open shells on either side casually displaying to any chance passers-by the peeling wallpapers and crumbling paint of their former glory, the place quickly became a target for all the town's vagrants.

They had tried to warn the old lady, all those engaged in trying to get her to move out, but she had stubbornly refused to listen. In the end, the council had wired off the access to the lower rooms on either side of her home and she had become resigned to living out the rest of her life in enforced solitude.

Alice had only thought of the jutting empty arms reaching out each side of her home as serving to protect her walls from the weather. It had never occurred either to her, nor the disgruntled council, that those arms could be made to tighten until they crushed away her liberty.

But then the footsteps had started.

'There's a lot to be said for being decently dressed when things like this happen.' Speaking aloud, Alice tried to console herself, a little ashamed of her recent terror as her courage began to return. 'Nothing is ever as bad when you're decent as it seems when you're caught in your nightclothes and such,' she earnestly informed the companionably ticking clock in an attempt to excuse her former cowardice. Maybe I'll have a word with Ginger if he looks in tomorrow, she promised herself silently. He's a

big strapping lad, he'll soon get things sorted out. Clinging to that crumb of comfort, she settled into the warmth
of her blankets to await the coming of daylight.

She was a tiny old woman, so tiny her frame scarcely
raised a bump under the fleecy pile of her bedclothes.
Never more than four feet ten or so, it seemed that age
had managed to shrink her fragile bones even further,
until now, as she entered her eighty-second year, her pro-
portions had become almost childlike. Only the grizzled
steel of her hair, losing its youthful curls to a thin, wispy
frizz, revealed that it was not, after all, a child curled in
the bed, for her skin, though creased with age and tissue-
fine, still retained a soft bloom that might have misled a
hasty glance.

The morning dawned cold and bleak with all the gloom
possible of late November. The icy draught creeping
under the door persuaded Alice to keep to her bed. 'At
least until the streets are aired,' she told herself, turning
painfully on arthritic hips. There was very little for her to
get out of bed for these days anyway, she reflected in an
uncustomary burst of depression. Only hours of sitting
alone hoping to hear the click of the door latch that
would tell her one of the children had dropped by.
Wasn't even a proper fire to keep her company no more,
she chafed, pulling the bedclothes up round her shoulders.
Only one o' them new-fangled gas things. Wish I'd never
let them talk me into having it fitted, blooming contrap-
tion. Her burst of resentment over, she lay watching her
breath making little puffs of vapour on the cold air, and
her mind drifted back, as it so often did now, to the days
of her childhood and the bitter cold of the winters she had
experienced then.

They hadn't been unhappy days, she concluded; in
spite of the poverty of those times, people had seemed to
stick together more then, help each other over the bad
bits, like. Theirs had been a large family, with nine sur-

viving children, and Alice the oldest. She and her four
sisters had all shared the same bed, sleeping three at the
top and two at the bottom, head to feet, feet to head, like
so many sardines in a can. Gone they were now, all the
rest, all gone barring herself.

The wars between them had taken her brothers and
tuberculosis had claimed the two youngest girls. Alice
sighed and eased herself into a more comfortable position. Long ago on days like today, when the hard frost
pinched, she and her sisters would crawl from their
enveloping nest in the thick flock mattress to find great
forests of beautiful trees etched by the night frost on the
glass in the windows. They would laugh and squeal
together in childish excitement, their bare feet stung by
the cold as they fled over icy linoleum. Nor was there ever
any rush to be first to plunge warm hands into the freezing water held by the ewer, Alice recalled. And the
scramble to get into their clothes after making a show of
washing the sleep from their faces in the great china bowl
would produce more squeals and arguments as undergarments were snatched and re-snatched between them.

As the eldest, Alice had to see after the others, helping
them into their flannel petticoats, buttoning through the
endless rubber buttons down the fronts of thick, fleecy
bodices which were donned in September and ne'er cast
aside until the proverbial May should be out. Why, she
could even recall herself being stitched into a red flannel
bodice that had encased her bony child's chest all one
long winter after she'd had a bad go of the croup. With a
wry smile twisting her lips Alice pursued her memories.
When the girls were all dressed, down the stairs they
would go to sit with their brothers, toasting their toes
around the black iron range while they ate their breakfast
bowls of warm milk and bread. If their father was home
he would take a penny from the vase on the mantel and
make peep-holes for them by warming it on the bars of

the range before pressing it to the ice on the windowpane. Always wanted his penny back, though, Alice remembered. Had to have it too, to pay for the bit of scrag-end or maybe a lump of fat belly-pork that would take them all through the week with food in their bellies.

'Aye, it wasn't only the winters were hard in them days,' Alice told herself. Not with nine growing children all needing to be fed and clothed out of a railwayman's wage. 'And that was when he was lucky enough to be drawing a wage,' she added softly before paper-thin lids slid over eyes looking far into the past. Alice sighed once before drifting slowly back into sleep.

Short though the days were at that time of the year, Alice found this one long enough to ponder the happenings of the previous night when she at last rose and dressed. She had felt she could cope with being the only resident left in the now silent streets, could even put up with the vagrants making use of the empty houses each side, but this business of someone or something creeping about in the dark hours of the night was upsetting her badly. The shriek of the wind as it played about the empty chimney had her starting up in alarm, and she shuffled around her cramped living-room in restless agitation.

'Hiya, Ma. How are yer today, then?' The bright carroty head was thrust into the room like a banner.

The loud cheerful greeting, bursting in on the old lady's sombre thoughts, arrested her stumbling tread as she crossed the hearth.

'Oh, good heavens, Ginger, you did make me jump. I didn't hear you come in.' Alice turned carefully with the aid of her walking-frame until she faced the tall, wide-shouldered youth who had now entered the room and stood by her table absently picking currants from the slice of fruit cake she'd laid out for her tea. 'Would you like a bit of cake, lad? There's plenty left.'

'No thanks, Ma. Just thought I'd look in, see if you was okay.' Ginger licked a sticky smear of cake from the end of his finger and grinned at her disarmingly. A fuzz of red hair blurred the outline of his rather slack jaw and sprouted just long enough at the corners of his baby-full lips to curl in a wispy parody of the moustache he was so desperately trying to grow.

'None of the others bin round today?' he asked, drying his finger down the front of his anorak.

'Not yet they haven't, and I suppose it's getting a bit late like, now.'

Alice concentrated all her efforts into working her way round the room to her chair, her joints creaking audibly with every step. Her armchair stood with its back to the room's narrow window. Leather-covered and high, with an upright back and hard padded seat, it had never been built for any real comfort, but she had bought it years back when she and her Sid had first set up home, and now the shiny worn leather allowed her to slip in and out of it without too much effort. Clinging with one hand to her walking-frame, Alice groped for its nearer arm, balancing her weight between the two as she carefully lowered herself into a sitting position.

'I was going to ask you —' she nodded towards the youth as she recovered her breath — 'if you would mind taking a look upstairs for me, Ginger, please.'

'Upstairs?' The boy's voice was breaking, and the word rose and quivered like a budding soprano's first note. 'What, now, d'yer mean?' The words dropped back down the scale.

'Well, if only you would, lad. You see . . .' Alice paused, a little afraid the lad might think she'd gone daft when he heard what she had to say. Then she went on resolutely, 'You see, I, er, I heard somebody up there last night. Footsteps, like. Creepy footsteps, sort of.'

'Garrn! Nobody can get up there without comin'

through here. And there ain't nobody done that, now, is they?' Ginger switched from stout denial to the affected manner of an adult trying to humour a child. 'Or are you holdin' out on me?' he crooned. 'Got a bit of spare on the side?'

'Not at my age, I haven't.' Alice grinned up at him, quite amused to be teased in this way. 'So could you just have a look for me, son? Don't want none of them there squatters and such.'

'Well, okay. But I don't suppose it'll be any use.' Ginger crossed the small sitting-room in a couple of strides and Alice heard him mounting the wooden stairs that rose steeply between the room she now sat in and the one at the front of the house, the one that had once been her best parlour, but which had now been called on to serve as her bedroom since she could no longer manage the stairs.

'Can't see nothink up here,' Ginger's voice echoed down the stairwell. 'I'll just take a gleg in the back.'

Footsteps clomped through the overhead room and crossed the upper landing. 'Nah, nothink in here, neither.' With a clatter he dropped down the stairs two at a time and bounced back into the room. 'There's nobody bin up there, Ma. Not fer years,' he reported, making elaborate show of dusting his hands. 'Yer must 'ave bin hearing things.'

'No, I'm sure I wasn't. There was definitely something up there last night.'

'Nah, must 'ave bin from one of them empties next door. P'raps the wind or somethin'. Could 'ave bin one of them tramps come back again, like.'

'I don't think so, Ginger. The sounds were coming from one of my empty rooms, straight overhead they were, not next door,' Alice began to argue. But seeing Ginger set his chin in a stubborn tilt she gave in and said with a resigned sigh, 'Oh, well. Probably you're right. Perhaps it was only the wind. . . Must have been wearing boots, though,' she attempted to joke. ' 'Cos it was certainly loud enough to keep me awake.'

'That's it! That's it, then.' Ginger's face registered a brilliant conclusion. 'It was a cat. Must 'ave bin.'

'A cat? But . . .'

'Don't you see, Ma? It was you sayin' about the boots that gave me the clue. Puss in boots, and all that. Course, I know it probably sounded like somebody walkin' about to you down here, well it would, wouldn't it? But I'll bet you what you like it was a bloomin' old moggie.'

'I suppose it could have been,' Alice said doubtfully. 'If you are sure there is nothing else to be seen.'

' 'Course it was.' Ginger's reassuring tone was heavily overdone and he sauntered towards the outer door as if anxious to avoid any further discussion of the subject. 'I'll be off now, then. Don't want ter be late tonight. I'm takin' my girl to the flicks tonight.' He spoke the last sentence loudly in a burst of childish pride and defiance that went oddly with his well-developed physique.

Alice smiled at him fondly. There was a special place in her heart for this fifteen-year-old man-child whose wits sometimes lagged behind the mature shell of his body.

'Ooh, taking a young lady out, are you? Better pass me my purse, lad.' She nodded towards the high mantel. 'If you're going courting all at once you'd best be doing it proper.' She extracted a pound note from the folds of her purse and held it towards the boy. 'There, how will that suit?'

'Oh, thanks, Ma. That's smashing.' He stuffed the note into his pocket and gave her a bashful grin. 'I'll bring her round ter meet yer, if yer like.'

'That would be nice, Ginger. I'll look forward to it. Just don't leave it too long, will you?'

'P'raps not tonight though, eh? P'raps later?' He edged closer to the door, suddenly afraid that he'd offered too much. He'd never before had a girl-friend and he wasn't sure at this stage in their relationship how his bright, sparkling Freda would take to coming out to meet a housebound old woman. He thought he'd better sound her out first, make sure it was okay.

Some of his anxiety conveyed itself to Alice, who said encouragingly, 'Of course not tonight, lad. You'll want a bit of time to yourselves before you start visiting folks. Now off you go, don't keep her waiting.'

Alice shooed the boy on his way with a playful wave of her hand.

She listened as his footsteps crossed the back yard and receded down the tunnel-like entry which separated the lower rooms of her house from those of the house to her left. The sound, ringing and careless, served to emphasize the secrecy and stealth that had cushioned those she remembered of the night before. Because, no matter what Ginger said about cats and so on, Alice was convinced it had been footsteps she'd heard last night. And footsteps of someone up to no good, at that. Ah well — she gave herself a little shake and squared her shoulders — it wouldn't do to brood. Now then, what had she been doing before Ginger came? Oh yes, she was just going to make herself a nice cup of tea.

Gathering her strength, she wriggled forward out of the chair and began the laborious business of getting herself across the room to the kitchen. While she waited for the kettle to boil she leaned against the chipped porcelain sink and stared through the window at the empty kitchen standing mirror-fashion opposite her own. A nice young family had lived in that house last. Just one youngster they'd had. A little boy, Mark. He used to play marbles on the blue bricks paving the back yard, just like her own boys had when they were small.

The family had moved out now, of course. Same as the rest of her neighbours, moved out by the council, they'd been, when they started this redevelopment business. Lot of new-fangled nonsense, Alice thought. Pulling down perfectly good houses. Well, she wouldn't let them pull her house down, that she wouldn't. Came here as a bride, didn't she? Her and her Sid, and it had always been their home. She couldn't imagine living anywhere else. It was very old, she'd never denied that, and a bit inconvenient with the lavvy being outside, but just the same it was home. And it was here she would stay, footsteps or no footsteps, she told herself firmly as she poured boiling water into the teapot.

CHAPTER 2

Nothing had disturbed Alice that night. If her nocturnal visitors paid her a call she slept on unawares, waking long after her usual time the following day. She was in the act of dressing herself when a sharp rap at her door jolted her out of the concentration she always applied to the business of making the hooks meet the eyes of her corset fastenings.

'Who is it?' she called, scarcely expecting to recognize anyone making reply, since all her regular visitors knew well enough to use the back door.

'Welfare Department, Mrs Maxwell. May I come in?' answered a female voice.

Alice froze in the act of pulling the two sides of her corset together. Welfare! Her heart gave a sickening lurch. Had they come to make her move out, like they'd tried once before? She remained silent in her sudden anxiety, her fingers gripping tighter at the flesh-coloured satin while her breath caught in her throat.

'Mrs Maxwell?' Her unseen visitor shivered out on the street, wondering what kept the old lady from answering.

'Go . . . go round the back, the door's open,' Alice found her voice and her courage. 'I will be through in a mo.' She let the remaining fastenings swing open; there would be time to struggle with them later. Right now she needed to get into her dress.

The tap of heels rang down the entry, then a polite knock sounded from the back of the house only moments before the door was pushed open.

'I shan't be much longer, just sit yourself down and make yourself comfy,' called Alice, doing her best to dress herself with reasonable speed.

'Please take your time, Mrs Maxwell. I don't mind waiting,' came the accommodating reply.

In spite of all Alice's efforts to hurry, a full ten minutes passed before she was ready to greet her caller.

'I'm sorry,' she said as she hobbled into the room, 'But I can't get around very fast any more.'

'That's quite all right, Mrs Maxwell.' The Welfare Officer, a pleasant-featured young woman Alice guessed to be in her mid-twenties, offered her hand. 'I'm Betty Kent.' She fished in her handbag and produced an identity card. 'I'm the visiting officer for this district and I thought I'd just call to see how you are—if you need any help from the department.'

Alice released her grip on the walking-frame long enough to acknowledge the introduction, returning her hand to take up its hold with the least possible delay. Then, when she saw how her movements were being studied, she made a tremendous effort to minimize her dependence on the frame's support.

'I'm just out of bed,' she explained, attempting to cover her weakness. 'I'm a lot better once I get myself going.' Whatever the cost, she couldn't let them think she was too feeble to look after herself. She didn't want to be pushed into one o' them there homes for the rest of her days.

'I'm sure you are fine.' The younger woman smiled. 'I

only called to let you know I'm about in the district and to tell you I'm available if you should need any help.'

'Well that's very kind of you,' said Alice, beginning to lose some of the defensive resentment she harboured against all officials. This girl seemed nice enough in all conscience, she decided.

There had been a man round to see her once, and he had come from the Welfare, although if she was to be honest Alice could never swear to that, since she was inclined to lump all those who had plagued her since the clearance scheme began under the collective heading of 'they'. *They* were the ones who had nearly frightened her to death with their forms and pages of jargon. *They* were the ones who never seemed to know about ordinary folks like her. *They* lived aloft somewhere, above the trials and tribulations that beset the rest of the world's population. *They* had the power to push folks around, order them here and there, tear down their houses, dig up their streets, and all without so much as a by-your-leave. *They* were all-powerful, *they* were, and a group to be feared, so Alice had learned to be wary when any of their minions found their way to her back door.

The man *they* sent had tried to fool her with his soft-voiced approach but she could tell that he thought her a stupid old woman for all his smooth words. And her conviction had been borne out by the way he had narrowed his lips and slapped his papers back into the black brief-case when she had refused to be taken in by his smarmy assurance that he only had her welfare at heart.

His footsteps had clanged away down the entry like so many angry words of reproach. But she had stayed in her chair until her heart stopped its silly fluttering, then she had taken a steadying breath and told herself firmly that she was not going to be bullied into doing anything she did not want to do. It was all well and good for *them*, but she was too old to make changes.

Was this young woman sitting here so innocently going to be another of them? she wondered, eyeing her dubiously.

'We are concerned about you, you know,' she told Alice now. 'Living alone in these conditions can't be very easy.'

'What conditions might that be?' All the old lady's suspicions came flooding back, lending an edge to her voice. They'd sent this girl here to wheedle her way in. Next they'd be sending others, to trap her. Make out she wasn't fit to live on her own! Cart her off like a load of useless old rubbish!

'Oh, please. I meant no offence. I only meant it must be difficult being without close neighbours.' Betty Kent hastened to placate Alice. 'But I can see you are quite comfortable here, quite able to manage alone.'

'I'm not alone. Well, not really alone. The children call in most days, you see.'

'The children? Oh, I see.' The words were drawn out as if the speaker was indeed witness to some revelation. 'In that case, Mrs Maxwell, there's no need for me to trouble you. I was under the impression that you were . . . were . . . well, alone in the world. But if you have children in close contact then you'll hardly be needing me.'

'That's right, but it was kind of you to come anyway,' said Alice. 'Shall I see you to the door?' she offered quickly, aware that she had inadvertently given the girl a lie and anxious to see her on her way before she could be caught out.

'No. No. Don't trouble, Mrs Maxwell. There's really no need, but thanks all the same. Goodbye now, and take care.'

'Goodbye,' echoed Alice, envying the mobile ease with which her visitor caught up her bag and gloves from the table before letting herself out.

Once she was alone Alice gave herself up to the worry

and apprehension the unexpected visit had caused. Who had set the Welfare on to her? Why had they come? She didn't believe all that twaddle about just calling to see if she was all right. Stood to reason they were up to something, once they knocked at your door. Well, she'd told them once, and she'd tell them again. She wasn't about to give up her home. Not after spending near on sixty years in it, she wasn't. All the same, it was lucky she had mentioned the children. Perhaps they'd think twice about trying to make her move out if they thought she had someone of her own to back her up.

Would have had, too, she thought sadly. If it hadn't been for the war. My Cyril was a lad any mum would be proud of. He'd soon have told them where to get off. Her eyes misted over the loss that none of the intervening long years could make any easier to bear. Fell at Dunkirk. Alice sighed. Eighteen years old and he 'fell at Dunkirk'. Alice had never been able to express the sick, haunting misery those three words evoked. She had never quite been able to imagine her eldest lying in peace, not with those words in her mind. He was always shell-torn and bloody. The khaki he'd worn so proudly, dirty and sea-stained where he'd lain in the mud and the sand.

And there had been Amy, she thought, twitching her mind from its harrowing picture to one of more gentle regret. A picture at sixteen months old and just beginning to talk. Thought it would kill Sid when we lost her. Adored her, he did. And he couldn't fight back against her killers, not like he'd done for the boy. There had been no weapons to use against diphtheria in those days. A tremulous sigh left Alice's lips, bearing as much regret for the grief of her husband as for the loss of their child. Only Georgie was left. Too young to go soldiering in the war that robbed him of his brother. He'd grown up in a time of ration books and blackouts, and nights spent singing 'Ten Green Bottles' down dank-smelling air-raid shelters with the rest of the neighbourhood children.

Perhaps it was the unrest of those early days, followed by the compulsory two-year spell of National Service, that had made Georgie unable to settle. In any event, it seemed to Alice he'd scarcely climbed out of his uniform before he began talking about emigration, and off to Australia he had gone. He was married now, to a girl he'd met over there. He still wrote, of course, but with four youngsters to raise he'd never been able to save enough to make a trip back home. Nearly thirty years it was now since he went over there. Some place just outside Adelaide. Alice frowned in concentration. Aye, but it was funny to think of him as a grown man. Just a lad of twenty or so he'd been when he left. And she and Sid still young enough to believe the promises they made each other, that they would all meet again. Maybe over there, Georgie said. Once he'd got settled and made enough to be able to send for them.

What a time that had been, the week Georgie sailed. Sid had taken a holiday from work and they'd gone to Southampton to see Georgie board the ship that was to take him across the world. Alice couldn't get over how big it had been. She had never imagined a ship of that size. Fancy a great thing like that being able to float. They had watched her sail on the morning tide, staring after her long past the time when they could clearly see anything but a smudge in the far distance.

'Come on, old girl. Let's go and get a cup of tea.' Sid blew his nose and swallowed twice before he could manage to hold his voice steady. 'There's a nice little café just out of the docks. A good strong cuppa is just what we need.'

'Sid?' Tears trembled in Alice's voice.

'What, love?'

'Do you suppose they drink tea in Australia?'

'Bound to. And if they don't, we'll take 'em a pound or

two when we go.'

'Yes. Yes, we'll do that.' Alice felt cheered, reassured by Sid's confident promise. She managed a watery smile and, tucking her arm into his, kept pace with his steady tread as they made their way from the dock.

A series of scuffles and thuds sounding along the outside wall snatched Alice back from the past. She barely had time to register the noise as heralding the children's arrival before the back door burst open to spill a plethora of arms, legs, and feet by her chair.

'Eh, eh, eh. Steady, now. Are you three fighting again?' asked Alice unnecessarily.

The tangle of limbs sorted themselves out and three children began yelling in mounting crescendo, each anxious to lay the blame on the others for starting their fight.

'It was all his fault.' John, his spiky brown hair contrasting sharply with the tow-coloured heads of his opponents, lashed a wild punch.

'Oh no it wa'n't.' The punch was skilfully parried by the only girl of the trio, speaking in defence of the smaller boy, whose features and colouring proclaimed him clearly her brother.

'Aw, why don't yer go and boil yer head, four-eyes!' The vehement jibe sent a fresh rain of blows flying indiscriminately between them.

'Now stop it. Stop it at once!' The authoritative voice, unused now for many a year, issued from Alice, so surprising the combatants they immediately did as they were ordered. Alice surveyed them in silence for a moment or so, knowing better than to ask for the cause of their quarrel.

John, Elaine's senior by several months, being only two weeks short of his tenth birthday, was nearly a head taller than the other two. And had the grace to return Alice's gaze with a shamefaced, almost apologetic air. Elaine tilted her head defiantly as she watched him, her grey eyes hard behind the thick lenses of her spectacles. While her brother, Tony, a sturdy eight-year-old, possessed of a pleasant, open face, grinned disarmingly round them all in general before tucking his warm, dimpled hand into Alice's.

She couldn't resist an answering smile and patted his hand lovingly before saying, 'There. That's better. Now one of you pass me the biscuit barrel and let's have no more of it.'

'I'll get it. I'll get it.' The girl pushed both boys aside in her rush to the cupboard that was built into the alcove formed by the deep chimneybreast. An overweight child, she trundled the short length of the hearthrug with a cumbersome, thigh-rubbing gait. Reaching inside the cupboard, she found the old-fashioned biscuit barrel and drew it towards her. Hugging it close to her chest, she lifted the lid and groped with a dirty hand into its depths.

'Hey, Ma. Stop her. She'll pinch all the best.' With a shriek of protest her brother launched himself at the girl and clawed for the barrel.

'Now then, Elaine. Share them out, there's a good girl. Tony and John want some too.'

'Here, then.' Grabbing a fistful of biscuits for herself, Elaine pushed the barrel at Tony, who proved too slow seizing his chance, and John scooped the prize before his outstretched fingers could grasp it. When he too had made his selection he handed the barrel on without speaking. Bulging cheeks and busy jaws demanded a truce of them for the time being, and Alice, indulgently watching their obvious enjoyment, was reminded that she'd eaten nothing since rising.

As she reached for her walking-frame and began pulling herself to her feet John swallowed his mouthful of biscuit to ask quickly, 'Where are you goin'?'

'Oh, don't fret. I'm not running away. Just going to

make a swallow of tea for myself. Missed my breakfast today.'

'Why did you?' The brown eyes fixed enquiringly on her face reminded Alice of the little mongrel pup they'd had when Georgie was small. She smiled and reached to ruffle the spiky hair. John was a bit like a neglected puppy, she thought, brown eyes, tumbled hair, and feet too big for the still-growing legs.

'Why did I?' she said in reply to his question. 'Why, because the blooming Welfare was here before I was out of me bed.'

'The Welfare!' She had their full attention now, and Elaine cut in before John could say any more.

'You don't want the Welfare hanging about, Ma. They put my Gran in a home, they did. She screamed all the time they were takin' her away. It was horrible.' The pink-framed spectacles glinted as she nodded her head to emphasize her words, and she paused knowingly before adding in sombre tones, 'She hadn't been there a month 'fore she died.'

'Well, they're not putting me in no home, and all this doesn't solve the problem of what I'm to have for my dinner,' declared Alice, in a brave attempt to banish the chill induced by the meaningful silence and the rather grisly picture conjured up by the fat child's statement.

'Can I stay for my dinner today?' pleaded John, fixing those begging brown eyes on her face. 'Me Mam's at work till six an' I can't get into the house.'

'Yes, of course you can, son. But I don't know what we shall have.'

'And us,' shouted Elaine. 'Can me'n Tony stay as well?'

'But what about your Mam? Won't she be expecting you home? And anyway, now I come to think of it, why aren't you all at school?'

'It's holidays, and our Mam won't care,' answered Tony, discarding the now empty biscuit barrel.

'Holidays,' echoed Alice. 'What for this time? Teacher's rest?'

'Nah, half-term,' supplied John.

'Half-term? Why, you haven't been back five minutes since the last lot. Half-term, indeed. Got some fancy names for things these days, I must say. Why I mind the time . . .' Her voice trailed away, as it so often did when she got caught up in her thoughts.

'Tell us, Ma.' A hand tugged at her sleeve. The children loved to hear her tales from the past, finding most of them greatly diverting.

'Eh?' Her eyes lost their faraway look as they focused on the faces turned expectantly to hers. 'Oh, there's nothing much to tell. I was just thinking about the days my Georgie used to get off school to go spud-picking.'

'What? Spud-picking?' The children exchanged nudges and grins. This was really something new.

'That's right. It was the war that did it. Wasn't enough men left at home to see to the farms, so he used to get let off school, about the middle of October it would be, and he used to go picking spuds on the farms around here. Used to be a lot of farms round abouts here in them days.'

'Did he get paid?'

' 'Course he did. Sometimes got as much as a florin.'

'What's a florin?'

Alice looked at Tony suspiciously. 'Are you acting silly?' she asked.

'No,' he protested with an injured air. 'I don't know what a . . . a . . . what you said, is. Do I?'

'Then it's time you did. A florin's two shillings.' There was no enlightenment on the children's faces. 'Two shillings, you know. Two bob.' Alice stared from one to the other in exasperation. They grinned sheepishly, none of them wishing to admit to being none the wiser. In the end, Elaine asked defensively.

'How many pence is it?'

'Pence? Twenty-four, isn't it? Twelve pence one shilling, so two shillings would be twenty-four.'

'Oh. Well, why didn't you say twenty-four pence then, in the first place.' Elaine was indignant.

'Because we always called it a florin,' said Alice with finality.

'Well, I don't think that's very much money for picking spuds,' said John, losing interest in the subject. 'What will we be having for dinner?'

'We can have beans on toast, or egg on toast, or there's a tin of stewed steak. I could do some potatoes with it, to make it go round,' Alice offered from the door of the pantry, where she'd made her way to see what its shelves had to offer.

'Yuck! I don't want any of them. Can't we have some chips?' asked Elaine to a chorus of approval from Tony and John.

'I don't think I've got enough taters for chips,' said Alice doubtfully.

'No. I mean chip-shop chips. Bought ones, you know.'

'Well, that would make a change.' Alice stood for a moment in thought. 'Pass me my purse, let's see what money I've got.'

'You've got plenty of money, you have, haven't you, Ma?' John stated confidently as he passed over the purse.

'Eeh, I wish I had, son,' Alice sifted through the coins she'd taken from the purse with a doubtful expression. 'I'll have to part with my last bit of silver. Still, it's pension day tomorrow, so I won't starve till then.' Making a roll of the coins, she looked enquiringly towards the children. 'Now who's going to go for the chips?'

'I will, if I can have a fritter for going,' offered Elaine, and the other two immediately wanted the same.

'Sorry. I can't run to fritters for all of you, so I think we'd better let Elaine go since she's the only girl. You two can have fritters next time, when I've got more money.'

'But why haven't you got any money now? My Dad says you must have loads if you can pay for a taxi just to pick up your pension.' John was scornfully emphatic.

'How else would I get it? I can't walk all the way into town and I can't get on a bus, so I have to have a taxi since missus next door moved away. Isn't anybody else to fetch it for me now.'

'Can I come with you next time? I've never been in a taxi.' John's eyes were begging again.

'We'll see,' said Alice, reluctant to make any promises she might have to break. She didn't know if she'd have to pay extra if John went along and she couldn't afford to spend any more than she need.

'We'll all come.' Elaine spoke with confidence. 'We'll go and get your pension, then we'll go to the pictures, and we'll have toffee and ice-cream, then we'll buy some cakes and bring 'em back here for our teas.'

'And who is going to pay for all that?' Alice asked weakly.

'You are, of course.'

There was something in the tone of the voice, or was it maybe the peculiar light in the grey eyes, narrowed by the thick lenses, that caused a chill hand to grasp Alice's heart. Looking, bewildered, from one to the other of their three faces she had an inexplicable feeling that she had just been threatened.

CHAPTER 3

Her uneasy feeling persisted, although nothing further was said by the children, who spent the afternoon playing a riotous game of snap until the early darkness wrapping itself about the house caused Alice to urge them to be on their way home.

'There's no street lamps round here now, you know, and I don't like you wandering about in the dark.'

'Let's just have one more game,' begged John, reluctant to return to a home where he was either constantly ordered this way and that, or completely ignored while his mother attended to the new baby.

It had been all right at home before that stupid baby came. He mouthed bitter condemnation of its existence whenever he saw his mother take it up in her arms. It had been fun when there was just him and his mum and dad. But not now.

Now, his mum made him see himself off to school while she looked after the stupid baby. Then she took it in its pram to a crèche on her way out to work, and collected it again on her way home. That left no time for the games she used to play with him when she met him out of school. Now he had to go home alone; she said he was too big to be met now, anyway. All because of that rotten, stupid baby, John decided. Who wanted the useless, bawling thing in the first place? Not him. And not his dad either. Because he went out to the pub every night since it came and John had heard him telling Mam if she wasn't careful he'd find somebody else to take care of his needs.

John had hoped he could be that one. He'd begun by following his dad wherever he went. Dogging his heels like a shadow until his father, feeling reproached by the silent, wide-eyed boy, had rounded upon him, ordering him to get from under his feet and act his bloody age. Hurt and bewildered, John had taken his revenge by inflicting sly little nips and pinches to the tender flesh of his baby sister.

It had taken his parents some time to discover the cause of the sharp purple bruises peppering their daughter's limbs, but when they had his father had coldly and systematically pinched John in return. Stinging his arms and legs until the boy sobbed that he would never do it again.

After that John took to spending all his free time with Tony and Elaine. They'd brought him along when they came to see Alice and it was here he'd met Ginger, and later on Paul, the undisputed leader of their little band.

It was because of their eagerness to waylay Paul that Tony and his sister turned a deaf ear to John's request for another game of cards, though they were curiously careful not to say as much within Alice's hearing.

'No. We can't stay any longer,' Elaine declared throwing the cards in a heap. 'There's something on the telly I want to see.'

'Yeah! Hey, yeah.' Tony seized on his sister's excuse admiringly and leaped to his feet in his eagerness to back her up. 'Got to go now, or we'll be too late,' he said loudly, flinging his arms into his coat as he turned towards the doors. 'Tarrah, Ma,' he called towards Alice as the other two followed his lead. 'See you some time termorrer p'raps.'

'Well, mind how you go then. And shut the door behind you,' Alice called after them, too late to have her request met with. 'I don't know, born in a barn all three of them,' she grumbled aloud as she made to get up and go to close it herself. Her progress was so laboured she had barely reached it when it was pushed from under her hand by a small wiry boy in a hurry to make his way in.

'Why, hello, Paul. Could have saved myself a job,' she said ruefully. 'Come away in, you have only just missed the others.'

'Yeah, I know. I seen 'em in the street.' Dark, narrow eyes swept over her and the young-old face wore a curious expression as it gazed into her own. 'What's the Welfare bin here for?' he demanded.

'Welfare? Good Lord, how did . . . Oh, did the others tell you?' She didn't wait for his reply but went on comfortably, 'I don't know, lad. Trying to find some excuse to make me move out, I shouldn't wonder. Not that it'll work, whatever it is.'

The eyes narrowed even further. 'You didn't *ask* them to come, then?'

'Who, me? You must be joking. I don't want them poking about, do I?'

'No, 'course you don't. Like you said, they only want to make you move out,' the boy said stiffly.

'Well, are you coming or going, then?' asked Alice. 'It's too cold to stand clacking with the door open.'

'I'm coming, for a few minutes, anyway.'

'That's right, lad. Come and have a warm.' Alice creaked her way back into the living-room.

Paul closed the door and followed her in to stand as close to the burning gas-fire as comfort would allow. Tearing a spill of paper from a dog-eared magazine lying on the table, he thrust it into the flame and withdrew it to light a cigarette.

'You know, you really shouldn't . . .' began Alice, then, catching sight of the way the boy's face tightened, she changed her admonishment, to add, 'be out so late these dark nights. What time is it, anyway?' Oh dear, another error, she really ought to know better. The boy was semi-illiterate and unable to tell the time by the clock. There existed a sort of unspoken agreement between them all that he should never become aware that they knew of this failing, and here she was, blundering along like the old fool she was. She hastened to cover her error. 'It'll be on the wireless if you just switch it on. I think the clock's wrong anyway.'

'Where is the wireless?' Paul asked sullenly, the blood rising in an angry line along the prominent bones of his cheeks.

'On there, look, the sideboard, right under your nose.' Alice spoke lightly, desperately trying to introduce a jocular tone, she hadn't meant to hurt the boy's feelings.

'Huh. No wonder I couldn't find it, you've got too

much junk on here.' Paul lifted a battered transistor from its niche amongst the vases and candlesticks jostling for position on the lacy runner covering the top of the crowded sideboard, and began fiddling with the knobs.

'Pass it to me, love. I'll sort it out.' Alice reached for the set and the boy extended it in her direction, only to let it drop inches short of her outstretched hands. Alice's sharp cry of shock and protest was lost in the crash it made striking the floor.

'Whoops. Butterfingers.' An unpleasant smirk replaced the boy's former tight-lipped expression as he saw in Alice's face a measure of the hurt he'd inflicted. 'Well, never is much on the radio these days,' he observed. 'Bet yer won't miss it.'

Alice stared up at him, helpless tears pricking her eyes. The little radio was the only bit of company she had, apart from the children.

She had thought herself extremely modern and chic when she'd bought it, her old floor-standing set having given out after more than thirty years of service. She had seen the youngsters in the street with their little modern sets, a plastic plug stuck in one of their ears, as often as not, while they jumped and twitched to their favourite sounds, and she had been fascinated by them. The wireless had been quite a big innovation in her young life, with the first lump of crystal, and the wire probe they had called the cat's-whisker. Then they had been improved upon and she and Sid had bought a set that needed a thing called an accumulator which had mysteriously been recharged at a local shop whenever she had trundled the weight of it there resting across the bottom of the baby's pram.

Sid had enjoyed that set. He used to listen to the football matches on it with the aid of a printed, numbered pitch which was issued along with the daily paper.

'Square six, section two. And now the ball is sent

towards the defending goal. Square ten, section three.'
The commentator's directions had helped bring the
added excitement of seeing how the game was going
along with his verbal description. She and Sid, like most
of their friends, had made little counters that they moved
backwards and forwards over the paper pitch to the commentator's directions. She couldn't remember when that
form of commentary had been discontinued, but she did
remember Sid's proud grin when he'd presented her with
the shining walnut cabinet that housed the latest valved
set. How different the tinny, sexless voices had sounded
on that, and how close, almost as if the speakers were
actually in the room. All this passed through Alice's mind
as she mourned the little transistor, and the tears welled.

'Oh, don't start scratin', I'll get yer another. It was an
accident, wasn't it?'

Alice continued to stare at him, too shaken to think of
making any reply.

'Well, wa'nt it?' he shouted, his mouth so close she was
sprayed with his spittle.

'I . . . I . . . Yes. Yes, of course it was, Paul,' she
managed at last.

His hard accusing gaze beat down on the apologetically
lifted blue eyes for a long, long moment before he turned
and flung out of the house, banging the doors to behind
him.

The taxi, booked on a permanent basis, arrived promptly
at the appointed time of eleven a.m. the following day.
Alice had been up and dressed and waiting since eight.
The business with Paul had upset her, keeping her awake
most of the night as she worried and fretted over his
alarming behaviour. She had actually been afraid of him.
She couldn't understand herself, and the more she
thought about it, the less she understood the very real fear
that had gripped her when the child had turned on her.

After all he *was* only a child, she kept assuring herself. A little underfed, undergrown child at that. But no matter how she strove to belittle her fear by playing down the size of her adversary, Alice could not rid herself of the uneasiness his attack had provoked. Paul was a different type of child from the others, she knew; quick-witted and sharp and possessing an underlying sensitivity, he went to great lengths to keep hidden. Alice had sensed this side of his nature from their first meeting and had played along with the tough-guy image he affected only because he constantly withdrew from any softer approach.

Under this ruthless veneer, Alice was sure, lay a child in desperate need of love and affection. Sometimes, when he had turned up at her home late at night after the others were gone, it seemed he would unbend a little, drop his shield of aggression, and accept the affection she was waiting to give. Once, he had opened up enough to tell her something of himself and the life he lived with his mother and a succession of 'uncles' in their flat on the top floor of a high-rise block. Alice had been genuinely interested. She'd seen the blocks being built some years before, though she'd never ventured inside. There were some aspects of daily life in those new-fangled things that had always intrigued her. And Paul had been self-important over his ability to put her straight about some of her more curious imaginings.

'But how do you get to the dustbins?' she had asked. 'Going up and down all them stairs would be enough to kill a horse. And don't tell me you have lifts 'cause I know you have lifts. Don't like the blooming things either. So how do you go on?'

'There's a chute,' said Paul, enjoying this chance of airing his knowledge. 'On each landing there's this cupboard thing, see? And you put all yer rubbish in that.'

'And who empties that, then?'

'Nobody. It just sort of empties itself.'

Alice pondered this statement for some time, then decided Paul must be having her on.

'You'd better make me one, then,' she said with a laugh 'I could do with a dustbin that empties itself.'

Shortly after that evening Paul's mother took a new 'uncle' home and Paul hadn't come round to see Alice for a while. She had learned about the new paramour from Ginger, who begged her not to let on that he'd told. When Paul reappeared at her home, the sullen lines around his mouth had deepened and he rejected all Alice's attempts at a welcome. That was when he started calling her Ma. Before that it had always been Mrs Maxwell, nice as you please, but now it seemed he must hide his dependence on her friendship behind some form of disrespect, so it became rather slightingly, Ma.

The other children, after some hesitation, followed his lead, and soon Alice came to accept it, familiarity clouding its harshness and bringing a measure of affection to the name, though the warmth once poised to grow between her and Paul had never returned. And it would seem from his manner of the previous evening that he was now going to treat her with this new and frightening hostility. Well, she would see about that, Alice had told herself throughout the long night. She wasn't going to let him scare her to death; all the same, she didn't feel overbrave as she sat, turning the whole thing over yet again in her weary mind, while she awaited the arrival of the taxi.

When Ron, the driver, tapped his usual tattoo on his hooter she was tempted to tell him she wasn't feeling quite up to going out today, and would he come as usual the following week? Then, taking a grip on her ebbing courage, she struggled to her feet. I'm just being a silly old woman, she chided herself. Letting my nerves get on top of me. But in spite of the way she berated her own lack of spirit she couldn't help being conscious of a certain relief when she opened the door and saw Ron's friendly, smiling face.

'Hello, Mrs M. How are we today?' Ron took her arm and helped her across the crooked paving-slabs before easing her gently into his cab. 'You look a bit peaky, old love.'

'I — Oh, no, Ron. I'm fine.' For a brief moment Alice was tempted to tell him her fears, to pour them all out and see what he made of them, but she didn't want him to think she was going a bit queer. People did, she knew, when they lived all alone. So she held her tongue.

'I see. Too many late nights, then, is it? Been out on the tiles?' When his jocular quizzing brought no response Ron cast a keen glance at his elderly fare. Say what she likes, he decided, she's not her usual self today, and that is a fact.

Unaware of his scrutiny, Alice stared sightlessly ahead. Fretting herself with the thought that perhaps she really was going to pieces. What with hearing footsteps in the night, and now this . . . this ridiculous state she had got herself into over nothing more than the naughtiness most children were apt to display at some time or another.

'Here we are then, love.' Ron's voice broke the unaccustomed silence between them. As he pulled into the kerb by the Post Office he gave her another keen glance. 'Look here, are you sure you're all right?' he asked worriedly.

'Yes, Ron. Thanks. Don't worry about me. I'll be right as rain once I get round the shops. I'll look for you as usual out by the clock.'

'Well, take it steady, then,' Ron ordered needlessly, his anxiety blinding him to the grim humour of his remark, applied as it was to an old lady physically incapable of moving any quicker than a snail's pace. He helped her from the cab and marked her slow progress as she moved with the aid of her walking-frame towards the Post Office. His brows drew together in a worried frown. She was too old to be going about on her own. Must be all of eighty, and crippled at that. Having watched her out of sight, he slid behind the driving wheel, let in the clutch, and moved off into the string of traffic. Following his normal routine, he'd returned later to the clock tower on the other side of the shopping centre, to collect Alice and take her out to the cemetery before running her home.

This weekly trip to the Post Office and shops had become the highlight of Alice's life. First, she collected her pension and an airmail letter form to write to her Georgie, then she'd set off along the covered walk through the shops, where she would entertain herself nicely taking stock of the latest fashions displayed by the boutiques and remembering the days when she had been young enough to crave a bit of glamour and a few colourful dresses for herself. Wouldn't have done though, she reminded herself ruefully. She'd been in service when she was a girl and her clothes had been supplied as part of her salary. Two outfits a year, she'd been given, one for winter and one for summer, along with six white aprons, and she'd been lucky at that. Most girls at that time had to be content with one new dress every twelve months or so, and a weekly wage of three shillings, which didn't leave much over for fripperies. So black or grey it had to be, with only a starched white collar for a bit of trimming. These flower-strewn and spangled affairs so pretty on the youngsters today had not been for the likes of her. Still, she'd had clothes enough once she'd wed her Sid, and she drew great enjoyment now from the colourful window displays.

On she went, working her way across the centre until she reached the supermarket, whose windows gave on to the exit and the square housing the clock tower she was making for. Alice had patronized this store when it had been no more than a two-counter grocery. Now it was one of the biggest privately owned supermarkets in the

Midlands, she'd been told. But that didn't mean it forgot its old customers. There was always a welcome for Alice from the girl in the tobacco booth and she'd signal a girl from the packing department in the back of the store to come and attend to the old lady.

It had long ago been arranged that she would leave her written grocery order on one Thursday and collect it completed on the next. Time was when a cheeky-faced errand boy would run it round to her home on his carrier bike, and be more than pleased if she tipped him a sixpence. But those days were gone now, of course.

'Don't know how I'd go on if it wasn't for this little arrangement,' Alice was at pains to tell the kindly assistant, who was old enough to share some of her old customer's memories. 'Can't think how other folks manage.'

'Oh, they've all got their own cars these days, Mrs Maxwell,' the assistant would inevitably reply. 'They don't believe in waiting about to be served now, you know.'

'No. Well,' and Alice would sigh, half in despair of a world that had accelerated too quickly for its older generations to keep up, and half in bewilderment that neither young nor old seemed to know or care for the simple delights of the other.

CHAPTER 4

A cheery pip-pip on the cab hooter warned Alice that Ron had returned, and she made her farewells to the supermarket staff in time to meet him at the door as he came to pick up the small cardboard box containing her week's supply of groceries.

'I must say that your little outing seems to have perked you up a bit,' he said in approval as he tucked her into the cab.

'Yes. Told you it would. Got myself a bit morbid, that's all. You know how you do sometimes when you are all by yourself.'

'Why don't you move out? Get yourself a nice little bungalow, one of those with a warden to keep an eye on things for you?'

'Not likely. They're not sticking me in no council-run gaol. A friend of mine had one, some years ago now, mind, but she said she couldn't even scratch her nose without asking permission.'

'But they can't all be like that, and look how you're fixed now. No neighbours, no friends living close enough to pop round for an hour or two. You must feel very lonely with all the rest of the street gone.' Ron spoke without much hope of convincing his passenger. They had argued over this problem before and he knew Alice could be very stubborn when she chose.

Once again Alice was tempted to take him into her confidence regarding the change in the children's manner towards her. Surely he of all people would be able to understand and advise. Then, as the words rose to her tongue, she swallowed them resolutely. No, perhaps it would be better not. 'Aye, lonely I might be, and lonely I am at times if truth be known,' she substituted for her intended burst of confidence. 'But I'd rather be lonely than beholden to other folks for the roof over my head.' She spoke with such finality Ron gave up with a smile and a shake of his head.

'I don't know,' he said mournfully. 'There's been no holding some folk since women's lib.'

'I'll give 'em women's lib all right,' Alice laughed in the cracked cackle age had made of her once infectious chuckle. 'Can't say I ever saw the point in burning none of my unmentionables, though.'

'Go on, Mrs M. Bet you were a real goer in your younger days,' Ron teased as he steered his way through the elaborate one-way system that would put him on the ring road in the direction of the cemetery.

'You know, Ron,' Alice was serious now, 'we never even thought of such things as bras when I was a girl. Bust bodices we wore to keep us trim and tidy. Didn't have no mucky talk of breasts and things in them days. No, and none of them there rapist fellas either. So it just goes to show.' What exactly 'it' went to show Ron was never informed because he drew to a halt at the cemetery gates just as Alice ended her speech.

'Now don't go standing about in the cold,' he called after her as she worked her way laboriously towards the flowerseller, standing well muffled and blowing on his fingers where they protruded past the end of his half-gloves. Baskets of tulips and tight daffodil buds lay at his feet, while seasonal wreaths of holly and laurel were propped against the sooty brick wall rising behind him.

'Pick me a nice couple of bunches,' begged Alice, indicating the tulips and proffering a pound note.

'Not for a pound, love, I can't. Sixty pence each today, I'm afraid. Time of the year, you know,' he hastened to add as he saw the consternation on Alice's face.

'Why don't you take a wreath?' he asked kindly. 'It would stay nice right through till Christmas, then if the weather gets bad, you won't need to come.'

'Oh, but I must come,' Alice exclaimed. 'Wouldn't be right not to bring a few flowers.' She added another note to the one in her hand and received her bunches of tulips along with the change.

The flowerseller stamped his feet to restore circulation and shrugged his greatcoat up round his ears. His eyes, watering in the cold wind, followed Alice's progress as she struggled to cover the short distance along the raised path to the white headstone marking the grassy plot where she held weekly communion with the man she had loved. As she reached her goal and bowed her head, the flowerseller turned away in respect of her privacy. His gaze went to Ron, who returned the unspoken salute to the old lady's devotion with an imperceptible nod of his head.

Ron allowed a few minutes to pass, then left his taxi to cross in a few quick strides the distance that had asked so much endurance of Alice. Taking the flowers from her fingers, he stooped to place them in the square marble vase that had the names Sydney, Cyril and Amy engraved in gold, one to each side. The only blank face was turned away from the path and he was glad of it. Though not an over-imaginative man, the smooth, unmarked space always seemed to him to be waiting, as if impatient for the addition of one more female name to complete its broken pattern.

'Come away now, love.' He touched Alice's arm. 'Let's get you home out of this cold.'

Hefting the box of groceries in the crook of his arm, Ron waited while Alice unlocked her front door. 'What have you bought all these biscuits for, Mrs M?' he asked idly, glancing over the contents in the box. 'Got a sweet tooth, like?'

'No, not me. They're for the children, Ron. I like to give them a bit of a treat.'

'Seems to me you treat them a bit too often,' he said disgustedly, following Alice into the house. 'I'm sure you've got better things to do with your bit of pension than blue it on a load of spoiled kids.'

'Now, Ron. They're not spoiled, not really. And I haven't got a deal else to spend it on, you know.'

'And not a deal to spend either, I suspect.' Ron shook his head reprovingly. 'I don't know, Mrs M. I've seen those kids you're on about and they all look better fed than you do to me.'

'Aye, well. Mebbe they do, but they're a bit of company, and I don't mind buying a few biscuits now and again.'

'Suit yourself, love. Only don't let 'em come it too

regular,' he warned.

'I won't lad. I won't,' promised Alice as she paid him the pound note he took as his fare. She was not to know, for he wouldn't hurt her pride by telling her, that this wouldn't so much as cover his petrol expenses. He had became very fond of his elderly charge during the months he'd ferried her backwards and forwards, and had privately decided on a figure of payment he thought she could afford without arousing any suspicion in her that he was offering charity.

'See you next week then, shall I? Same time as usual,' she asked now.

'Sure enough, Mrs M.' Ron paused on his way out and turned to survey Alice doubtfully. He always felt a little reluctant to leave the old lady alone in this house, and today the feeling became even stronger. 'You'll be all right, then?'

'Yes, thanks, Ron. Now don't you worry about me,' Alice urged, and had the satisfaction of seeing his encouraging smile before he turned back to the door.

Alone in the pleasant warmth shed by the gas-fire, her purchases carefully put away, Alice drowsed in her chair. Must get a bit of cleaning done tomorrow, she promised herself. Can't abide a mucky house. But she was too tired to contemplate making the effort just now. I'll just open a small tin of fruit as a little treat for my tea, then I'll be off to my bed, she planned.

It wasn't until after this promised feast, when she picked up the little radio to take along with her for company, that the worry she had felt over Paul's attitude returned with a sharp little stab. Losing her radio was like losing a friend. She didn't care much for television, couldn't understand more than half the things they put on anyway, and though she used to enjoy a nice read, her eyesight wasn't so good any more. 'I'll just have to see if I can't get you mended,' she informed the radio without a great deal of hope, for it rattled alarmingly when it was tilted.

In spite of feeling so weary Alice found it difficult to sleep. Must be a bit overtired, she thought, thumping her pillow and easing her position in an attempt to lessen the ache in her spine. Slowly, her muscles released their tension and she began to relax. Then, just as the pleasant weightlessness overtook her, she heard them again. Footsteps! She was sure of it, crossing the room overhead. With a swooping, sickening sensation she rushed back to full consciousness. She felt the hot sweat of fear start from her pores. 'No. Oh, no,' the whispered words formed a plea in the darkness. She couldn't bear any more of this nocturnal torture.

For a few weak moments Alice permitted all the nameless horrors of childhood to crowd through her mind. 'Oh God, help me. Help me.' She bit at her knuckles in utter distress. Was this how people went when they were queer in the head? her inner voice questioned. Hearing things? Afraid of the dark? Was that what was happening to her? Madness? Her spirit rose in rebellion. No! Never! No, not she. There had to be some explanation for the noises she kept hearing. It had to be squatters or some such. The thought gave her courage. Yes, that was it. Someone was living up there, in her empty rooms. Even so, it took all her resolve to draw her arm from the protective tent of her blankets and grope through the darkness towards her bedside lamp.

With a sigh of relief she found it, and her terror drew back like a snail with salt on its back as she depressed the button, creating a little oasis of light.

'Who is it? What are you doing up there?' she called, struggling to sit up in bed. 'I know what you're up to,' she informed her suspected listener, 'and if you don't get off I'll send for a bobby.' In the following silence Alice had the unmistakable feeling that her own questing ears were not the only pair striving to catch the slightest measure of sound. Feeling unequal to the task of leaving her bed to make any further investigation, she piled the pillows behind her shoulders and settled back, prepared to wait out whatever, or whoever, should be hiding above. Perversely now her eyelids grew heavy and she began to doze. Her last resolve on the brink of oblivion was to waste no further time before putting this whole business into the hands of the police.

In the room overhead Paul shot a look of angry contempt towards Ginger. 'Bloody fool,' he hissed, fury overcoming his self-imposed rule of silence. Ginger flushed a dull guilty red, making no attempt to move from his arrested position and keeping his eyes sullenly lowered as Alice's tremulous threat to call in a bobby brought further murderous shafts from his companion's narrow gaze. He stood as though frozen, knowing better than to make any move that would give further cause for Paul to round on him. Just when it seemed he could hold his strained position no longer a sharp 'pssst' drew his attention. A jerk of Paul's head ordered him to make his way out of the room, and he did so with all the stealth he could muster.

The younger boy then led the way down the rickety staircase of the empty shell sharing Alice's walls, and out through the ground-floor room to what had once been a garden. Clear of the danger of being overheard, Paul gave vent to his wrath.

'How many times do you need telling? You big stupid sod. Galloping about like a bloody overgrown ape. Do you think she's daft, or summat?'

Although twice the size of his angry companion, Ginger bore the tirade with the same guilty silence he had previously maintained. In no way placated by this, Paul continued to rave.

'I don't know why the hell I bother with you. You won't be satisfied till you get us all nicked.' At this Ginger mumbled some inaudible reply. 'What?' The narrow eyes pierced him. 'What did you say?'

'I said, there's not much chance of that.'

'Don't talk so wet. You heard what she said about calling the rozzers.'

'How can she?' Ginger was sure enough of his ground now to offer an argument.

'How the hell do you think? She just goes out and asks one of 'em ter take a butchers up them stairs, you twit.'

'She can't get out, though, can she? Not to go anywhere, I mean. And if she asks one of us—well.' Ginger shrugged negligently.

'Look, stupid. What's ter stop her askin' that taxi ter call at the station?'

A widening of Ginger's eyes revealed that he hadn't considered this possibility.

'See? I keep tellin' yer. We're on to a good thing providin' we keep the old girl from guessing, but once she finds out . . .' Paul left it to Ginger to puzzle the outcome of that eventuality for himself.

'I'll come and see her tomorrow, cover up, like,' he offered at last, anxious to make amends for his stupidity.

'Oh no you won't. I'll be the one that comes ter see her tomorrow, if anybody does,' Paul assured him with heavy emphasis.

Alice slept late the following morning and had some difficulty at first in recalling the events of the night. That she had some need of help was her waking thought, but then she couldn't quite be sure what had prompted it. As she went about the slow business of getting herself washed and dressed, the last rags of sleep cleared from her brain. Memory rushed back, making her pause, one arm upraised in the act of drawing a comb through her sparse hair. Yes. That was it. She had it now. Those footsteps again.

'I'll have to get it stopped.' She spoke aloud to her

reflection in the mirror hanging over the mantel. 'Can't have folks coming and going just as they please, that I can't.' Her hair arranged to satisfaction, she put an egg to boil for her breakfast, then went in search of pen and paper. If she was to write a note for the bobby, maybe one of the children would take it round to the police station for her.

Composing the note and writing it out in her beautiful copperplate script took up most of the morning. Her hands had lost their suppleness, making her grip of the pen difficult to maintain, but it was finished at last, and she propped it on the mantel with a satisfied sigh.

'There now, that's done. Can't do no more until one of the youngsters comes in.'

There was to be no strain on her patience, for Ginger and Paul appeared before she'd had time to be aware of the waiting. They walked into her sitting-room together, Ginger subdued and unusually quiet, hardly speaking a greeting. Paul trod beside him like a wraith, his sharp, narrow gaze taking a sweep round the room before coming to rest on Alice's face with an expression that caused her to glance nervously in Ginger's direction. Ginger shuffled his feet uncomfortably as he lowered his eyes and pretended an interest in the floral tablecloth.

'Hello, Ma. How're you today, then?' Paul's voice was pleasant, and his manner so friendly Alice stared at him in surprise.

Had she only imagined the malice he'd extended towards her such a short time ago?

'I . . . I'm fine, love. Fine,' she managed to say, with only a slight tremor to betray her unease.

'Sleep well, did yer?' Again a friendly enquiry.

'I . . . No. No, I didn't.' Indignation helped push aside her nervousness as she went on to explain. 'I heard them footsteps again. You know, Ginger, footsteps like I told you about the other day? Well, I've decided to ask the bobby to come and have a look around.'

'Bobby!' Paul hissed at her. 'What are you talking about, woman? What bobby?'

Alice shrank away from the swift savageness unmistakable now in his face.

'Who have you seen? What have you said, you stupid old bugger?' Paul caught Alice's wrist in a grip of iron.

'N—Nothing. No one. Oh, Paul, you're hurting.' The grip grew even more painful. 'I wrote a letter. There! See?' Alice nodded wildly towards the mantelpiece as a sob of pain escaped her. 'It's just a note to the police.'

CHAPTER 5

The old lady's quivering statement clutched the two boys by the throat.

'Here!' Paul released his captive with a push that set her tottering and grabbing wildly, frantically, at her frame for support. Ignoring her difficulties, Paul snatched up the note and thrust it towards Ginger.

'What's this all about?' He spoke through clenched teeth.

Before Ginger could take hold of the paper, the back door was thrust open to admit Tony, John and Elaine.

'Hiyah, Paul. Hi, Ginger. Thought you two were going to see Steve.' Elaine paused as she crossed the room's threshold, caught by the drama of the tableau before her.

'What's that, Ginger? What you got there?' John pushed impatiently past her ample figure, his eyes fixed on the note that Ginger was now turning over and over in a helpless sort of fashion.

'Shut your gob, and wait to see,' Paul bawled, frowning fiercely in the direction of the newcomers, who refused to be intimidated by his obvious anger and continued to surge forwards.

As they moved into the room, Tony treading John's heels in an effort to see what was happening, their eager glances were drawn towards Alice. She was openly in a state of some distress. What had they been missing?

'Get on with it then, Ginger. Don't take all bloody day, read it, for Christ's sake,' Paul ordered.

Alice groped her way over to her chair and lowered her shaking body gratefully between its protective arms. She stared apprehensively towards Ginger, who sent her an apologetic glance before making a hesitant effort to unfold the note.

'Pissing hell! Will you get on and read the bloody thing?' Paul was almost dancing with impatience and rage.

Ginger began, 'Dear Sir. I . . . have . . . been . . . tr . . . trouble . . . d'

'Oh, give it to Paul, you dunce.' Elaine snatched the paper from Ginger's fingers and poked it towards Paul. 'Here, you tell us what it says.'

'But you know he can't read.' Alice bit her tongue, regretting her words instantly.

'Shut up, you daft old bag. 'Course I can read. It's you that can't write, you stupid old cow.' His face tightened murderously, and he punched Elaine's hand savagely to one side as he rounded on Alice. The others caught their breath as they watched his raised fist. Alice cowered against the back of her chair, terror robbing her of the power of protest. Only Elaine remained unaware of the mounting tension. Bringing the note close to her eyes she read it through to herself, mouthing the words silently before she waved it vigorously to attract Paul's attention.

'Hey, see here. It's a letter to the cops.' Her startled cry brought Paul whipping round.

'I know it's to the cops, stupid. What does it say?'

'She's askin' them to send somebody round. She wants them to look in the rooms up the stairs.'

All eyes swivelled to Alice. Gripping the arms of her chair, she stared wordlessly back into their five accusing faces.

'Why did you do that, Ma? Thought you was our friend.' John broke the silence, his liquid brown eyes seeming to convey a personal sorrow at this betrayal.

'Yeah. Thought you liked us comin' round here,' put in Elaine.

'I did . . . I do . . . I . . . the note, it isn't . . . I . . . .' Slow understanding dawning at last brought Alice no comfort. 'You mean . . . it was *you* up there? Up the stairs? Walking about in the night?'

' 'Sright, Ma.' Elaine's spectacles flashed pinpoints of light as she nodded at Alice. 'It was us all the time. Well, some of us, anyway.' Her high-pitched giggle held no genuine mirth.

'Shut up.' Paul thumped the girl spitefully between the shoulder blades. 'She knows enough as it is.'

'And what if she does? Can't tell nobody, can she?' Ginger spoke in defence of Alice. 'Ain't as if she's goin' anywhere.'

'That's right, Paul.' Eager to restore Paul to good humour, Elaine backed Ginger up loudly. 'She can't do nothing we don't want her to,' she crowed.

A ripple of understanding brought whoops of triumph in its wake as each of them reached the same delighted conclusion.

'What about her pension, and the taxi, and that?' Paul's question crushed their rising spirits.

But only for the time it took for Elaine to suggest, 'I could always go with her. Say she was feeling poorly and needed me, like.'

'Anyway, it's ages to pension day yet,' observed Tony. 'She went yesterday.'

At his words a calculating gleam was kindled in Paul's narrow eyes.

'Yeah, and that reminds me,' he said slowly, his eyes never leaving Alice's face. 'I'll be needing some bread seeing as how I've missed Steve. Where'd you put it, Ma?' His air of menace became intensified. 'Ma! Ma!' he yelled, as Alice made no sign that she had understood his demand.

'Eh? What? Put what?' she struggled towards comprehension.

'Your purse, you old fool. Where'd you put it?'

'In my bag,' Alice whispered obediently, lost now in this bewildering turn of events. She wanted only to be left alone. To be free to go about her daily affairs as always. Doing her bit of cleaning, maybe baking a cake or two in case the children fancied a piece. She couldn't understand all this anger and turmoil.

At Paul's insistence it was arranged that one or the other of them would always stay close to Alice. 'Don't want you getting any more bright ideas,' he told her, giving the leg of her chair a kick that jarred all the way up her spine. John watched, his brown eyes big and wide as he waited for some form of outcry from the figure hunched in the chair. Alice made no protest above a small, shocked whimper of pain.

'Me and Tony'll stay here today,' Elaine volunteered. 'You'll come back tonight though, won't you?' she asked Ginger and Paul anxiously.

'We'll be back about six. Now that she knows, we can bring all the stuff straight in through here.' Paul spoke over his shoulder, not troubling to look up from his search through Alice's handbag. 'Ah, here it is,' he extracted her old plastic purse. 'I'll just take a fiver, that should last me till we can shift some of the gear.'

'But that's my pension,' Alice was concerned enough to voice a protest. 'I shall need that. There's no more coming in till next Thursday.'

'What will you need it for, Ma?' Elaine nudged her brother and giggled. 'Going to the disco, are you?'

Tony rose to the cue, 'Nerr, she's off ter the boozer, goin' ter get pissed.'

'That's right.' Not wanting to be left out of the fun, John began staggering about in exaggerated imitation of a drunk, lurching violently into Alice's chair as he did so. Elaine and Tony were swift to join in.

Alice found herself plunged into nightmare. Her world had suddenly become peopled with grinning faces, yelling mouths, grasping hands and tumbling bodies that threatened to throw her bodily out of her chair.

'All right. Cut it out. Cut it out, I said!' Paul's voice rang to the rafters in an effort to rise over the din. 'Now listen, me and Ginger are off now. So don't let her out of your sight, and keep your eyes peeled, just in case.'

'What about givin' us some money, then?' Elaine motioned to the open purse Paul had tossed on to the table.

'Here, help yourself. But listen, don't go flashing it about,' he cautioned as he shepherded Ginger towards the door, 'and remember, if yer get caught, I ain't never set eyes on yer, either one. Understand?'

'Yeah, yeah.' Elaine snatched up the purse and held it aloft, out of reach of Tony and John's grabbing fingers, while Ginger and Paul disappeared through the door. Their going signalled pandemonium as the three younger children bit, fought, and clawed for possession of Alice's purse. Screaming and yelling, they thrashed about on the floor until their hurtling bodies crashed into Alice's chair. The edge of a shoe heel chopping down into the old lady's shin and her scream of pain brought an end to the fight. For a moment, the children were silenced, glances of shame and concern passing between them, unseen by Alice for the tears that flooded her cheeks.

Elaine was the first to recover her aplomb. 'Oh, what the hell. Serves her right, don't it? She started all this with that stupid letter,' she said with a ring of defiance.

'Yeah.' Tony surveyed the bent head pitilessly. 'Silly old bat. Here, who wants some money? Let's dish it out, shall we?'

'Not bloody likely. I want the money, I was the one that asked for it. So it's mine.' Elaine made a grab at her brother's arm.

'And I say we share it out, like Tony wants. That's two to one, four-eyes.' John glared at the girl, his fists clenched.

Elaine stared back at him only briefly before lowering her gaze. She gave Tony a nudge and said sullenly, 'Well, go on then, Tone. You've got the bugger. Dish it out.'

This time Alice made no protest as she watched the remains of her pension being divided into three separate lots. She felt too sick from the knock to her leg, and besides, the whole business had now slid beyond the realms of possibility. This couldn't be happening to her. The argument that developed over who was to be the one left behind, to watch over her, while the others went out to spend their portions of her pension raged about Alice completely unnoticed. As did their later comings and goings with their pockets bulging and stuffed to capacity with an assortment of sweets and comics. She was caught in the grip of a nightmare. Terrifying, formidable, and horribly, horribly menacing.

Slowly, as the children became immersed in their comics, the pulse of danger charging the small sitting-room began to ease. Crouched in her chair, teeth clenched against the throbbing pain from the slow-bleeding wound in her shin, Alice tried to puzzle out for herself why the children were behaving so badly. She had known them and loved them for such a long time; their sudden aggression towards her defied explanation. Why, she could remember the very day young Mark from next door had brought Elaine and Tony to meet her. Must be three, nearly four, years ago now. Elaine had been attending school for a year and Tony had just started going. That was how he'd come to meet Mark, they'd been in the same nursery class. Lovely babies they'd been, and so shy. But they'd opened up all right once they'd got a slab of her cake and a glass of pop in their hands.

When Mark and his parents had moved away, Tony and his sister had continued coming to see her, and they in their turn had brought John. Little John with his spaniel eyes and his lost expression. A smile passed unconsciously over Alice's face and she continued in her reverie. Ginger, of course, had been born just over the way, so he'd always been a regular visitor. Right from the time he could toddle. Only Paul, strangely cold and adult for the ten-year-old he was then, had come to her door uninvited. How he'd come she'd never quite known. She had been reluctant to probe, since any attempt to get close to the lad only resulted in his drawing back into himself. He was like a wild kitten, Alice had thought. Appealing in his loneliness, yet spitting and vicious if anyone tried to get close.

An urgent need to visit the toilet brought Alice back from her fruitless cogitations and she struggled to get to her feet. John and Elaine looked up from their comics as she rose, balancing herself with the walking-frame and trying to spare her injured leg.

'Where d'yer think you're going?' John asked sharply.

'Oh, don't worry. I'm not going far.' Alice moved painfully towards the back door.

'You're not going out.' John stepped across and took a grip on the frame, barring the way.

'Will you let go? I'm only going up the yard to the lavatory,' Alice was forced to explain.

John stepped aside but let his hand remain on the frame, undecided what to do next.

'You'd better go with her.' He jerked his head to summon Elaine.

'Aw, John. It's cold out there, and besides, I'm reading,' Elaine protested.

'I can go on my own,' Alice said, embarrassment pinking her cheeks. She hadn't been accompanied to the toilet since she'd been a child.

'No, you can't. Come on, Elaine. You'd better get moving, you know what Paul said.'

'Aaw.' Elaine threw her comic down and stomped to the door. 'Get shifting, then,' she ordered the flustered Alice. 'I ain't got all bloody day.'

Alice made her way without further protest through the back door and out over the blue bricks of the back yard, rimed now with frost. This was too ridiculous for words, she kept telling herself. It must be some sort of game they were all playing. It was only to be hoped they would soon tire of it.

'Come on. Be quick.' Elaine wrapped her arms about herself, shivering with cold. She shouldered open the toilet door and hopped from one leg to the other as she waited for Alice to make her slow way inside.

Struggling to manoeuvre her walking-frame in the small whitewashed cubicle, Alice became aware of the girl breathing down the back of her neck.

'Here,' she protested. 'You can't come inside.'

'What's it matter? I'm a girl, aren't I? Besides, it's too cold to stand outside.'

'Oh, Elaine. Please.' Alice gazed pleadingly into the bespectacled face. 'I'm going to the lavvy. Be a good girl and wait for me outside. I can't . . . can't go with you watching.'

'Oh, bloody hell. Anybody 'ud think I'd never seen a shit-house before.' Elaine barged heavily past the swaying figure clinging helplessly to the walking-frame, 'and don't take all sodding day or I'll come and pull the chain on yer.'

Alice shook her head in sheer disbelief. She just had to

be dreaming all this. Only, the worn wood of the lavatory seat, smooth and familiar against the back of her legs, seemed real enough. So did the throaty gush of water that came as she yanked the metal handle dangling from its chain.

Back in the house and safely installed in her chair, she watched the three children as they leafed through the pile of comics. They looked so innocent. So much the same. How could it be possible that they had robbed her, stolen her pension, and were even now acting as her gaolers? Occupied with their sweets and comics, Elaine and the boys left Alice in peace. But the short, dark day had drawn to its close long before Paul and Ginger got back, and they were restless now. Eager to be on their way home.

'D'yer reckon we should tie her ter the chair, and just go?' John's question struck a fresh spark of terror in Alice.

'We'll have to, if they don't get here in a bit,' Elaine was already nodding her agreement when the back door swung open and an icy blast preceded Ginger into the room.

'And about time, too,' Elaine's voice was strident as she rounded upon him, 'where the hell have yer been?'

'Busy.' Paul spoke from the shadows, giving Ginger no time to attempt a reply. 'You can get goin' now. We'll see to Ma.'

'Come on then, Tony. Leave yer comics here, we'll be coming tomorrow,' advised Elaine, her attitude becoming less assertive as she faced Paul.

'I think I'll stay,' said John, wetting his lips and glancing from Paul to Alice. 'Just for a bit,' he added hastily, seeing the angry frown his words conjured from Paul.

'Get off,' Paul jerked his head towards the door, 'and don't forget I shall want you here tomorrow.'

'Aw, shit!' John grabbed up a comic and made to slide past Paul on his way to the door. A quick and painful cuff to his head hurried his passage.

'Don't shoot yer mouth off at me.' Paul pushed him out into the night, slamming the door closed after him. Then, turning back into the room, he fixed a commanding eye on Alice.

'Time for bed, Ma,' he said. Alice stared up at him blankly. He drew nearer her chair. 'I said it's time for bed.'

'But . . . but, I haven't had my tea yet,' the old lady flustered.

'Too bad. Come on, I want you in bed.'

'Please, son. Let me stay. I won't do you no harm, and . . . and I'm hungry.' Weak tears slipped over the wrinkled cheeks.

'Let her stay, Paul. Like she says, she can't do us no harm.' Ginger looked from the huddled figure to his friend.

'No. I say she's safer in bed, out of our road, so come on.' He thrust the walking-frame at Alice and she gripped the familiar rails, trying to summon the strength to get to her feet.

'It's no use.' She let herself sag back in her chair. 'I've been sitting too long. I can't get my legs going.'

'Give us a hand, Ginger.' Paul ranged himself on Alice's left, indicating to Ginger to take his position on her right. 'Ready?' he asked. 'Then lift.' Between them they levered the bent old form to an upright position. So unequally matched in height were the two, they half lifted, half dragged their helpless burden through to the bedroom, where they deposited her on the bed with a careless thump.

Paul was red in the face and panting from the exertion, but he blustered around, determined not to let Ginger guess his lack of physical strength. He crossed to the front door and locked it, jiggling the handle before slipping the key into his pocket. He then drew the curtains across the window and paced back around the end of the bed towards the door leading out of the room.

'W-wait.' Alice gasped a lungful of air. 'Wait . . . Please.' She held a shaking hand outstretched. 'My frame . . . I . . . Please . . .' She lacked the strength to go on.

'What about it?' snapped Paul, suspicion leaping into his eyes.

'I shall need it.' Alice was steadier now, having fought down the worst of the pain the blundering journey had caused her.

'Not till termorrow yer won't.' Paul pushed Ginger through the doorway ahead of him.

'But . . . I sometimes need to get up in the night,' Alice made the confession barely above a whisper.

'Then you'll just have ter need, won't yer?' The reply was loud and positive. The bedroom door closing with a bang on the last word.

Alice stared after the boy in sick misery. It was no use pretending any longer that she was mistaken in the children's attitude towards her. The events of the day had made it only too plain that she stood in grave danger from their callous ministrations. But why? Why? was the question she kept asking herself, groping and fumbling through her memories to find some reason for their sudden hostility. She'd never done them any harm, never would, so why? Hadn't they always been made welcome in her home? Hadn't they been her only real friends since the neighbourhood had been demolished? Of course they had, so why? Why? Why? Alice rocked herself on the edge of the bed, her arms folded protectively about her narrow chest as tears of bewildered helplessness slid down her wrinkled cheeks.

They were afraid of her, that was the trouble. Not of her, Alice, exactly, but afraid that she would bring in some stronger authority to discipline and punish them.

But didn't they know they had only to ask and she would keep silent? She couldn't approve of their bad language, of course, and they would have to promise not to use it any more, but she didn't mind at all about them using her upstairs rooms, they were of no use to her these days anyway. Oh God. Didn't they know she would never have written that note in the first place if she had only known it was they who were up there. Couldn't they understand that?

CHAPTER 6

Once back in the living-room Ginger turned ponderously, his wrinkled brow betraying the effort his slow thoughts had cost him.

'Yer could have left her the frame, Paul. She won't do any harm,' he said.

'I've already told yer. I'm takin' no bloody chances. There's a good few quids' worth of stuff stashed away up them stairs, and if that nosey old bugger starts pokin' her snout in . . .'

'Why should she?' Ginger cut across Paul's angry speech. 'She never has before.'

'Never has before? Just hark at him.' Pushing his face into Ginger's he hissed, 'And who do yer think was going ter get the bloody police in, then?'

'But she didn't know,' Ginger argued weakly.

'No, she didn't know a lot of things. She didn't know it was us up them stairs then, neither. Well, she does now, an' it's no use you arguin'. She can stay where she is and do without the bloody frame. See?'

'But what if there's a fire or summat? She couldn't get out.'

Paul gave Ginger a long, measured look. 'Then she'd

just have to fry, wouldn't she?' he asked with quiet menace.

Mercifully, Alice heard nothing of this. Pushing herself up the bed to sit propped against the pillows, she tried not to give way to the nervous fear that had built up and was threatening now to overwhelm her. Deliberately, she made herself think along practical lines. She needed that walking-frame, that was the first priority, she was helpless without it. Slowly she began trying to massage some life back into her legs. The cut where John's shoe heel had caught her was swollen and angry-looking, and her thick lisle stocking, stuck in the congealed blood round the edge of the wound, pulled painfully each time she moved. It really ought to be bathed, she thought, impatient with herself now for not having seen to it when she had the chance. The thing was, of course, she hadn't wanted to draw the children's attention, having judged it safer to keep herself quietly in the background. And that had been something of a mistake, because for anyone with her complaint the trick was to keep on the move.

Arthritis could be the very devil once you let your joints set, she grumbled to herself, kneading carefully round the misshapen joint of her knee and pondering what she should do next.

She would have to talk to the children, make them understand how badly they were behaving. She realized, now that she had time to think about it, that she had stumbled on to some sort of secret. One so important to them they were prepared to go to great lengths in order to keep it. Somehow, she must persuade them that keeping her a prisoner simply wasn't necessary. She must ask them to release her. Maybe if she swore not to tell a living soul what she only half understood anyway, they would agree to leave her in peace. It was hardly a matter of life and death, in any case, was it? They had been very naughty indeed, but she could forgive them, and if they were using her upstairs rooms for some purpose of their own without having first asked her permission, well then, they should be thoroughly scolded, but after all, what did it really matter? She and her friends had used her dad's garden shed to keep their treasures in when they were young. Hung curtains up, she remembered, and made pictures for the walls out of old Christmas cards. It had been their very own private place, and woe betide anyone else who tried to get in.

She could recall still the smell of that old garden shed with the sun beating down on the roof, melting the resin in the boards and boiling the sticky black tar her dad had used to caulk them. Oh, they had been happy days all right before she'd had to leave home to go into service. Still, that hadn't been too bad, either. At least she had survived. Alice collected her wandering thoughts with a determined effort. She couldn't afford to sit dreaming of the past now.

It was *now*; she had to find some way to go on surviving, for she knew only too well that many more days like the one she'd just spent would surely end all her hopes of continued survival. By this time Alice had managed to convince herself that the children had no idea how serious their behaviour towards her had become. How could they be expected to understand the needs and the frailties of the old when they were so young and robust themselves? Perhaps if she explained carefully that she was too old to go on as they had today, then they would realize how thoughtless they had been. They would no doubt say they were sorry, and she would say it didn't matter, and they could all go back to their old happy relationship. Yes — Alice nodded approval of this plan — yes, that was the best way to deal with this thing.

Her contentment at having found a solution was of very short duration. What if they wouldn't listen to her? What then? Making no attempt to get undressed, she wriggled under the quilt and drew it up to her shoulders. She knew there was no use in trying to sleep, she was too upset and in too much discomfort for that. She had to think this thing through, cover every possibility, and find some foolproof way out of her present difficulties. Maybe she should simply escape. Get herself outside the house on the pretext of going to the lavvy, then just keep on going, over the back yard, down the entry, and off up the street. What could they do to prevent her? she asked herself with a desperate bravado, knowing only too well they had only to remove her walking-frame to render her helpless. And besides, it was much too far for her to walk in the time it would take for them to miss her, and maybe come chasing after, before she had reached any form of safety. Well, then, what if she pretended to be ill and in need of a doctor?

Alice felt her heart leap in excitement. Surely they would have to give up their restrictive vigil if that was the case; they wouldn't be prepared to spend day after day sitting by her bed, would they? And if they became worried enough to call in the doctor she could tell him what was going on, and ask him to help her.

On the other hand, she argued with herself, it might just suit them nicely if she was ill and confined to bed. They might be content to leave her there growing weaker and weaker; she would certainly be a prisoner then. No, no. She didn't dare try that. She would have to think of a better way.

Huddled in a woebegone bundle, Alice struggled over and over to make some plan of action, fighting to suppress the heartache the children's behaviour had caused her, lest she should lose sight of her immediate danger. She mustn't give way, she kept telling herself. It would help no one if she sat around weeping. Besides, there was no doubt things would look much better in the morning, she thought bravely. Things often did.

She rolled her head on the pillow, her headache adding to the bone-deep agony she was obliged to endure from the pain in her legs and hips. Her pain-killing tablets were on the bedside table but she had no water to help wash them down. She had heard Ginger and Paul leave some time ago and knew there was no use shouting for one of them to bring her a drink. Resolutely, forced by her pain, she shook a couple of tablets into her palm and slipped them into her mouth. Like burrs of gall they lodged in her throat, their bitter powder clinging to her dry mouth and tongue. Spiteful little pellets, they refused to dissolve, adding their own share of misery to the old lady's total discomfort.

By the time daylight lifted the oblong window into grey relief from the night-black walls, Alice had given up all attempt to make a plan of escape, concentrating instead on a heartfelt prayer for release from the tortures of her own pain-racked body.

The three younger children arrived in the middle of the morning. Alice heard their voices register surprise at finding her sitting-room empty. They came bursting through into her bedroom, springing the latch in its lock in their eagerness to find her.

'Why are you still in bed?' Tony and John spoke almost in unison.

'We thought you'd be in the other room,' added Elaine.

'Ginger forgot to leave me my walking-frame,' explained Alice, having decided not to put their loyalty to the test by having them know it was Paul's deliberate decision to leave her without means of getting about.

'Could one of you get it for me, please?' she asked now, scarcely daring to look in their direction lest they should see how desperately she was hoping they would meet her request. They eyed each other warily, not one of them willing to show any sign the other two could take as an indication that they were sympathetic towards Alice.

Alice held her breath as she waited. Tony lolled idly against the foot of the bed; he seemed not to have heard. John shrugged and turned away.

Finally, it was Elaine who gave way. 'Oh, I'll fetch it,' she said ungraciously. 'But don't think I'm going to be running about after you all the time.'

She returned to dump the frame by Alice's bed. Alice grasped the familiar metal thankfully, so pleased to have it once again in her possession her eyes brimmed. Getting down from the high bed and onto her feet took all the fortitude she could muster. Her joints had locked rigid, and every attempt she made to move them brought its own train of agony. The children watched her struggle with all the heartless curiosity of the very young.

'What are yer doin' with all yer clothes on?' asked Tony, as she freed her limbs of the clinging quilt.

'I was too tired to take them off,' lied Alice, thinking it best not to make any complaints. She didn't want them to turn on her again.

'Yer wasn't thinking of gettin' away in the night, was yer?' asked Elaine, giving her a sharp glance.

'No child, no. Good heavens, what will you think of next?' Alice spoke indulgently. If only she could persuade them she was a willing prisoner there might be a chance yet for her to get their relationship back on its old footing.

At last she managed to manoeuvre herself into a standing position. Clinging to the walking-frame and taking as much of her weight as she could on her arms, she began the tortuous journey from her bedroom through to the sitting-room at the back of the house. It took all her determination to make herself keep on the move. She knew once her joints had eased the pain would gradually lessen, but the stabbing torment of reaching that point was almost to much to bear. Stoically she struggled on, making slow, stumbling circuits of the small sitting-room until her efforts were rewarded and she could feel some of the stiffness beginning to ease. A nice cup of tea would work wonders, she thought, and began making her way back to her bedroom, intent on collecting the bottle of milk, which she had delivered daily, from the room's outside windowsill.

'Where are you goin'?' Elaine demanded, watching her narrowly as she reached the door letting on to the narrow hall at the foot of the stairs which she must cross in order to enter her bedroom.

'Only to get the milk, it'll be on the sill waiting.'

'Then let it wait,' Elaine's bulk brushed Alice aside as she charged past to slam the door closed.

Alice sighed and returned to the sitting-room to make her slow way from there through to the kitchen. She peered doubtfully into the milk jug she took from the cupboard.

'Needn't have worried,' she murmured beneath her breath, 'there's enough here to float a battleship. Would any of you like a cup of tea?' she asked sociably as she filled the kettle.

'Who wants rotten old tea?' Tony asked derisively. 'I'd rather have pop.'

'Yeah. That's an idea. Let's get some pop.' Elaine was enthusiastic.

'What with?' John's sarcastic enquiry brought a silence while brother and sister paused to consider the state of their finances.

'You got any dough left?' Elaine asked Tony without a great deal of hope.

'Nah — You?'

A disgusted shrug was the only reply he received.

'What about you?' he turned to John.

'I an't got any. Why don't you ask her?' He nodded towards Alice, who now emerged from the kitchen carrying a steaming teacup.

She glanced from one to the other of their expectant

faces and felt a stab of alarm. They'd taken all that was left of her pension only yesterday. She had no more to give.

'I . . . I . . . there's no more left till next week,' she stammered, clutching on to her frame with one hand, the teacup held in the other.

'Aw, come on, Ma. Don't tease.' John stepped closer to her, 'I mean, you've got plenty stashed away somewhere, I'll bet.'

'N-no. No, I haven't, John. You had all I'd got between you yesterday,' Alice looked despairingly at the threatening figure that was blocking the way to her chair. 'Please, I'll have to sit down,' she begged, her strength suddenly ebbing.

'Aw, go and sit down then.' Disappointed, John struck viciously at the full teacup, sending it spinning. A stream of scalding liquid arched across the room, spattering its other two occupants, who immediately sprang to outraged attack.

'Hey, you stupid bugger. That was me that fell on,' yelled Elaine, raining blows on John's head and shoulders.

'Yeah!' Tony joined in, 'why don't yer watch what ye're doin'?'

Alice backed into the nearest corner, holding her walking-frame to the front as a shield for her legs.

'Stop it. Stop it,' she implored, terrified that she would get pulled into the mill of flailing limbs. None of the combatants paid any heed to her quavering request and she shrank closer into the angle of the walls, her knuckles pressed to her lips.

It was only Ginger's timely arrival that put an end to the battle. He came bursting through the door, trailing the winter frost in the wake of his passage, and almost fell into the mêlée.

'Hey, what's going on?' he shouted, his big hand dabbing indiscriminately between the fighters, meting out sobering blows as he strove to pull them apart.

'It's him,' panted Tony, pointing an accusing finger at John, 'he threw boilin' hot tea all over me'n her,' his head jerked to include Elaine.

'Did yer?' Ginger asked curiously. 'What for?'

'Aw, take no notice of him. I didn't throw it. I knocked it, that's all.' John hunched his shoulders and slouched to a chair on the hearth.

Alice breathed a sobbing sigh of relief and made her way with hesitant steps towards the comparative safety of her own armchair. She'd do without her cup of tea for the time being.

'What's this all about, anyway?' asked Ginger, looking towards her with something like pity as his slow-moving brain took in her defensive withdrawal.

Alice glanced at him briefly before shaking her head. 'Nothing, lad. Nothing. I . . .' She paused. Then, taking courage from his sympathetic manner, forced herself to go on. 'I wish one of you would tell me why you are doing all this. I mean, we used to be such good pals, all of us, and now . . . I . . . you . . . they . . .' her voice trailed away as Ginger stared at her, uncomprehending.

'Pooh, take no notice of her, Ginger. She's just rab-bitin' on.' Elaine broke the uncomfortable silence, 'we an't done nothing, 'ave we?' The righteous disgust in her voice released John and Tony from their half-guilty listen-ing attitudes, and, as they rushed to add their voices in agreement, the moment for Alice to make an appeal for their understanding became lost.

'Well, that's all right, then,' said Ginger, happy to forgo any call on his powers of concentration. 'Anybody got a fag?' Patting his pockets he glanced hopefully around to be met with a look of scorn from Elaine that spoke for the three of them. 'Oh, well,' he shrugged. 'Paul'll be here soon. He'll have some, I s'pose.'

'What's Paul coming for?' asked John, bristling. 'Can't he trust us?'

'Nah, it's not that. He's goin' ter sort through some o' the stuff. Steve wants some specials. Christmas stuff, like.'

'Well, I think we should get more than a quid a week off Paul if he wants us ter look after her and keep stuff comin' in as well,' whined Elaine.

'Better tell *him* that, then,' said Ginger in a tone that left no doubt that he was not prepared to stick his own neck out. 'Any road, what do yer need cash for? Yer can allus nick what yer want.'

'Oh yes,' said John with sarcastic emphasis, 'we can allus nick what we want, but what about you? You never say no ter gettin' money, I've noticed.'

'Well, that's different.' Ginger turned his back on the angry boy.

'Why is it?'

'Yes. Why is it?' Tony and Elaine rounded on him now. 'Come on, tell us how it's any different fer you.'

'Well, I—I have ter pay fer things like, like pictures and stuff,' Ginger mumbled, shuffling his feet.

The three younger children whooped in derision.

'We know you've got a girl,' jeered Tony, 'we've seen yer kissin', so there!'

Ginger glanced guiltily across at Alice, the swift colour mounting his face until even his ears were a bright, glowing red.

But Alice was too busy grappling with her reeling thoughts to pay him much attention. Nick things? Nick what they want? Nick them? The slang expression and all its implications beat into her brain until she pushed away the horrible pictures forming behind her closed lids with an outward thrust of her hands.

The jolt of movement returned her to full awareness of the children's conversation in time to hear John saying, with deep conviction, '. . . and I reckon she's got a packet hidden away somewhere. Like under the bed or summat.'

'Yeah. Eh, yeah. I bet that's right, isn't it, Ma?' Elaine's podgy face shone with excitement as she turned towards Alice.

'Eh? What's that?' Alice struggled to keep abreast of this new situation.

'We was talkin' about all the dough you've got round here somewhere.' John's eyes travelled swiftly about the room as if he expected to find it festooned with pound notes.

'Let's look for it,' Tony urged, caught in the sudden urgency that seemed to be infecting them all. His words served as a signal for dispersal, with John and Elaine making in a rush for the bedroom while Tony turned his attention to the deep cupboard at the side of the fireplace.

Only Ginger remained, propping his hips against the side of the table and staring after them with a slightly dazed air.

CHAPTER 7

Alice retreated from the threatening bustle of activity into the sane and familiar safety of her past. Clutching the arms of her chair with shaking hands, she deliberately pushed away all the renewed fear and distress the morning had brought, and conjured up instead the happy warmth these four walls had held when she and Sid were newly wed.

Sid had been a twisthand in those days, an employment which made him both master and slave to the great steel machines that clanked away morning to night, turning uncountable cotton threads into the much-prized and beautiful Nottingham lace. He had been quite well off in comparison to most of his contemporaries, since he was frequently able to earn as much as five pounds a week, while they, lacking any close relations already in the trade to give them the edge it needed to gain this prestige occupation, had been obliged to seek lower-paid work wherever they could find it. As night soilmen, french polishers, stable hands and such, they were lucky if they drew as much as thirty shillings a week to take home. But Sid had to shoulder other responsibilities; besides his wife and young family, there had been his mother to support, along with three younger sisters, a maiden aunt, and his grandmother. His dad had died after an operation to correct a strangulating rupture he'd earned serving the very machines Sid now waited upon, and the duty of caring for the family's womenfolk had passed to his son, even as his mode of earning his living had done.

But they had been comfortable enough for all of that, Alice reflected happily. She had been taught how to make ends meet by her ever frugal mother and she had earned her husband's approval on many occasions by her never failing support. Things had been difficult for a time when their Cyril was born, for she had fallen victim to the 'white-leg' that meant enforced bed rest and the necessary payment of many doctor's bills, since she had made only a slow recovery. Even so, they had coped with a bit of pinching and scraping and the bit of money she had managed to put by.

'Have yer found owt yet?' Elaine's voice coming from the front room cut across Alice's dreams, reminding her that she wasn't alone.

'Nah, I don't think she's got owt.' Tony broke off his search of the cupboard long enough to send a glare of disappointed scorn in Alice's direction. His upper lip curled in a grimace as he added, 'There's no end of junk in this bloody cupboard.'

'Well, get sortin' it then, and don't chuck nowt out that looks interestin',' was Elaine's next command.

Alice stared mutely at Tony as he again busied himself in the cupboard, her pleasant reveries dispelled by the sound of their voices. Ginger remained propped against the table, his hands deep in his pockets, his gaze fixed unwaveringly into space. There seemed little point in making any appeal to him at this stage.

The pile of odds and ends, bits and pieces she'd been meaning to do something with sometime, continued to grow around Tony's feet. Her worn wooden darning mushroom rolled across the hearthrug. Well, hadn't she been searching for that only last week? Alice gave it a reproving glance before her eye was drawn by the soft gleam of crimson chenille lying in a little pool as it spilled from the cupboard. That was her old mantelpiece cover. Looked lovely, it did, with its bobbled fringe matching its twin tablecloth. Nowhere to put it now, of course. Not now the old iron grate was gone. And what a job that had been every week, cleaning and black-leading the boiler and oven, finishing off with a polishing rag dipped in vinegar to give it that extra bit of shine. Oh, but how proud she had been when it was done. These modern tiled affairs were never the same, Alice thought in disgust. What achievement was there to be had from just wiping a soapy cloth around?

'Hey, what's this?' Muffled by the confines of the cupboard, the question did little to draw the old lady's attention. 'Hey! I'm askin' yer. What yer got in here, then?'

This time Alice came back to herself with a start. Oh, no. Please. Don't let him find it, she prayed silently, her lips moving to frame the earnest plea.

If the children got hold of her careful savings she'd be finished. She wouldn't be able to pay her way and the council would then throw her out, she knew they would. She had never been in debt, never in all her life. Please don't let it happen now.

Her scrambled prayers were to be shortlived. And in vain.

'I've got it. Hey, you lot. I've found it.' Tony's voice shrilled from inside the cupboard. 'It's all in this old tin.' He drew his head and shoulders back into the room and triumphantly brandished a fistful of banknotes. The misshapen old tin fell to the floor with an empty clatter.

'What yer got? How much? How much is there, Tone?' The door from the stairway was thrust back into the room to meet with a resounding bang against the sideboard. Elaine rushed into the room, fat thighs rubbing one against the other and making a busy shh, shh, as she bustled across the hearth and crowded her brother into the corner. 'C'mon, tell me. Tell me how much you've got,' she demanded.

'Hey! Wait fer me, you two. I'm in on this an' all, yer know,' John yelled from the bedroom, his pounding footsteps telling of his rush to join them. He cannoned into the room, sending the returning door on another punishing trip to crash with the sideboard's edge. Ignoring Ginger, who had not moved from his slouched position by the table, he ploughed into the pair now grappling for possession of the money in the room's far corner.

'Ger away, you.' Elaine turned a broad shoulder on the boy, blocking his approach.

'You shurrup. I'm havin' my share of this lot.' John panted pushing wildly at the solid bulk of his opponent.

None of them paid any attention to Alice's cry of dismay.

'Leave it alone. It's mine, I found it.' Tony thrust his hands, still clutching the notes, into his armpits.

'I only want to know how much there is.' Elaine panted as she tugged at his sleeves, trying to prise his arms down.

'Gerroff, will yer?'

'Well, just let's see how much, will yer?'

'Nooo, yer big, greedy sod. Yer not goin' ter get it, so bugger off.' Bent almost double, the boy dodged past his sister, cannoned into John, knocking him aside as he fled from the house still clutching his treasure.

'I'll get him.' John made to follow but Elaine's hand shot out, grabbing him back by his hair.

'Oh, no, you won't. He's my brother; if anybody fetches him back I will.'

'Let go of me.' John's neck was strained backwards by Elaine's grip on his hair. He flailed wildly in her direction. She retaliated with a vicious tug to his head that broke her hold, and he rounded on her in earnest. Kicking, punching, and tumbling over each other, they fought to reach the door, and clattered outside in hot pursuit of the footsteps they could hear retreating down the street.

Ginger gaped soundlessly after them, trying to decide what action to take. Eventually he pushed himself upright and lumbered to the door, leaving Alice alone to stare in sick dismay at the fallen tin.

'They were my dues and demands,' she told the empty room in a broken whisper. 'What am I to do now?' Her eyes on the tin never wavered.

With a resounding crash the back door was flung open and John, coming in, cannoned into Ginger, propelling him back into the room to fetch up with a bang against the overcrowded sideboard.

Without waiting to recover his breath John immediately rounded on Alice.

'Why couldn't yer tell us where you kept it? Now that pig and his sister have collared the lot.'

'It was the rates money . . . and the electric . . . I'd been saving it up.' Hardly aware of the boy's presence Alice continued her fixed stare, seeing a prisonlike existence in some council-run home stretching coldly before her. Blindly she extended her hand.

'Please, the tin. Would you pass me the tin?'

'Why don't you stuff the tin up yer arse?' John mouthed viciously, stepping purposefully towards her chair. At her cry of alarm Ginger strode forwards and pushed him aside.

'Leave her alone. She didn't give it to Tony, did she? So leave her alone.' He bent and collected the tin, placing it gently on Alice's lap.

The gnarled fingers grasped it, swinging the hinged lid back into place. Softly they rubbed at the faded pictures, worn through in places to the metal below. King George in his coronation robes. Elizabeth, his queen, and on the other side, two little princesses, pretty as angels in their white organza dresses. The tin had started life as a tea caddy, one of the millions sold when the king had been crowned. There'd been a mug too, decorated with the royal coat of arms. One of her boys had been given it at school. She couldn't remember which of her boys it had been, now. But the mug had got broken some years ago. Well, the king had gone now, too. God rest him, and his brother, poor soul. Gave up his birthright for the love of a woman, and turned his back on a throne. Alice sighed deeply, remembering those momentous times. She wasn't aware that Paul had entered the house until his hand lashed out to send her tin, and her memories, crashing.

'I asked you how much there was.' Paul's voice was raised to a shout.

Alice stared up at him startled, still half lost in her dreams.

'The money, you daft old bag. The money! How much?'

'The money?' she echoed, unconsciously feeding his temper.

'Bloody hell, woman!' His fingers bit into her shoulders as he gave her a cruel, neck-snapping jerk. 'How many times do I have to ask?' he panted, thrusting Alice hard against the back of her chair.

Alice shook and trembled, fighting for breath. She raised one hand in a gesture that was both a plea to his mercy and a promise that she would answer as soon as she could. Finally she managed 'thirt . . . thirty-four . . . pounds.'

'Where's the rest?'

'No . . . rest . . . that's . . . that's all there was.'

As Paul reached out again, his grip tightening on her shoulders, her obvious terror convinced him of the truth of her words. He swung round to face Ginger.

'You stupid bastard. You let a kid of eight get away with the lot.'

'It wasn't my fault.'

'Of course it was, you dozy bugger. I told you to keep an eye on things, didn't I? Well, you can just wait now for him to come back, and when he does I'm going to murder the little snot.'

'Oh, please, please,' Alice begged, 'won't you please stop all this fighting and swearing?'

Neither Paul nor Ginger made any response. Only John, casting his eyes heavenward, betrayed that her plea had been heard. The four of them lapsed into a brooding silence until a pounding of feet in the entry forewarned of Elaine and Tony's return. They came breezing into the room, pockets stuffed and bulging, their arms hugging bottles of brightly coloured minerals.

'We've brought some stuff to keep us going,' Elaine declared, missing the malevolent gaze Paul turned upon them.

'Well, then, you'd best keep right on going.' Alice spoke up bravely, having decided she must put an end to this situation while she still had the strength. Only amazement at her affrontery held Paul in check as she continued. 'I may as well tell you, first as last, I don't want you to come here any more. None of you.' Alice gathered courage from their stunned silence and took a deep breath to steady her voice as she went on. 'I won't go telling any tales, if that's what you're worried about, but I want you to keep away.' She relaxed in her chair, glad to have the matter over and done.

The silence stretched on a full minute after her last word. Then Paul gave a wild screech of forced laughter.

'Listen to her. "I don't want you to come here any more. I want you to keep away",' he mimicked in a cruel parody of Alice's voice. ' "Why can't you play nicely, like good girls and boys?" ' His face twisted in an ugly snarl as he advanced upon Alice's chair. 'And what do you expect us to do then? Disappear? Oh, I forgot. You won't tell any tales, darling, will you?' He tapped her face lightly with the flat of his hand. 'Now, there's a good girl.' Again the tap, heavier this time, to emphasize his approval. Alice cowered away; drawing her head into her shoulders, she stared fearfully into the narrow face with its slitted eyes. She was already regretting the rash outburst that had drawn the boy's anger down on her head.

'You won't tell any tales, because I won't let you. So you can make your mind up to that, and we shall keep coming here just as long as it suits us. Do—you—see?' Each word was spaced with a sharp little slap to Alice's face.

The old lady stared up at her tormentor. With his slaps their roles had become reversed. Now she was the child, to endure whatever treatement this sadistic adult should feel fit to dole out. She shrank even lower into her chair but was unable to tear her eyes away from the dark slits boring down on her.

Satisfied with her submissive attitude, and conscious of the awe that had rendered his four companions silent throughout this little scene, Paul strutted a little as he crossed the hearthrug to stand with his back to the grate while he surveyed them each in turn.

'Now listen to me, you lot,' he ordered. 'Firstly, I want

three more trannies, and any cameras you can lay your
hands on. Jackson's have got a good lot in, they're right
away from the counter, and they aren't roped together
ner nothin', so there's where yer make a start. Now's the
time to make a killin'; what with Christmas comin' up we
should have us a bomb.'

'Yer mean *you* will,' said Elaine darkly, taking off her
specs and giving them a wipe on the front of her sweater,
as if to dissociate herself from the explosion she anticipated in reply.

'What? What did you say?' Paul's voice was danger-
ously quiet.

'Well, it's not fair. We only get a quid a week, and you
get all the rest. Even when we bring everything' yer want.'

'And who does all the work? All the runnin' about and
stuff?' asked Paul, speaking more in his normal voice. 'It's
not the nickin' that takes all the brains, yer know. It's the
gettin' rid that really counts.'

'Still, we ought ter get more than a measly quid,' Elaine
muttered, settling her spectacles back on her nose.

'And what would you do with it, yer stupid cow? Spend
it so's everybody starts askin' where you'd got it from? I
keep tellin' yer, it's safer this way. A pound each a week
fer comics and stuff, 'n' the rest hid away till we can make
up some good excuse fer havin' it.'

'I bet you'n Ginger have more'n a pound a week. Don't
yer?' Elaine persisted, her lips out-thrust and her podgy
face growing pink with indignation.

'Never mind what we have. We've got better reasons for
havin' us own money than you three kids.'

'Like what, fer instance?'

'Like havin' part-time jobs, fer instance.' Paul longed
to smash his fist into her accusing face, but he had
enough control to prevent him making an enemy of her at
this stage. Too much depended on her co-operation.

'Only Ginger's old enough to have a job. You're not.

You're only twelve.'

The girl grew bolder in the face of Paul's restraint, but this last taunt proved too much.

'Shut up! Shut up!' his voice rose to a scream, and he lunged towards her, grabbing a fistful of her clothing into a bunch at her neck.

'Yer can have one-fifty, and don't let me hear any more or I'll bloody well choke yer.'

Elaine clawed at the restricting lump, unable to breathe, her eyes rolling in fear behind the smudged glasses. With a sharp push Paul released her and shot a glance towards Tony and John, standing in apprehensive silence either side of their gasping companion.

'Anybody got owt ter say?' Paul demanded, and was satisfied when they both swung their heads in denial. 'C'mon, then, Ginger, let's go and take a gleg at the stuff.' He jerked his head towards the door and Ginger obediently led the way out.

Sitting forgotten in her chair, Alice had taken in the implications of the conversation with a growing sense of foreboding. If the children were all involved in some way with stealing from shops and so on, they were not going to give her the chance to pass on what she'd learned to an outsider. And what would become of her when they realized they couldn't stand guard over her forever, was the fear uppermost in her mind at the moment. She had to get away. Somehow, there must be an escape for her. Would it be any use appealing to one of the children? Away from the influence of the others? Or would that force them to treat her with even greater enmity than they were doing at present? She studied the three seated round the table. Could Elaine, as the only girl, be the one who might help her? Remembering how the girl had braved Paul's wrath for a bigger share of the profits, Alice thought it very unlikely. Tony and John she was forced to dismiss as being too much under Paul's domination. That left only Ginger. Big, slow, kindly Ginger. Yes. If she could only get him alone long enough to make him understand the danger she was in, she felt sure of enlisting his aid.

Having decided on asking Ginger for help, Alice was faced with the problem of getting him on his own. No use waiting for a chance opportunity, that might come too late, she thought grimly. No, she had to make it happen soon. But how? The sight of her teacup lying in shatters, where it had come to rest against the far wall, gave her an idea just as Paul and Ginger, arms laden, re-entered the room.

'Would . . . would anyone mind if I made myself a cup of tea?' she asked diffidently of the room at large. 'I . . . er . . . the last one got spilled.'

All eyes turned towards Paul, whose puny chest swelled visibly at the new importance of his role. He shrugged negligently.

'Get one if you want,' he told her, dropping the bundle he carried in an untidy heap on the table.

Alice struggled to rise, her hopes leaping. Perhaps this wouldn't be so difficult after all. Hanging on to her walking-frame, she shuffled into the kitchen where she filled the kettle and set it to boil before taking the half-filled milk jug and deliberately pouring its contents away down the sink.

'Anyone else like a cup?' she called through the open door, purposely keeping her voice light and pleasant. The success of her plan depended, she knew on retaining their old friendly acceptance over the space of the next few minutes.

'I'll have one, Ma,' called Ginger, coming to the open door to watch her pour out.

Alice could have kissed him, so neatly had he fallen in with her plans. She gave him a smile before looking deliberately about her.

'Oh, dear,' she said, voicing the lines she had so carefully been rehearsing in the back of her mind. 'I haven't collected the milk yet today. Come and open the window for me, son, will you? I always have the milk left on the front windowsill. Saves me bending, you see.' Alice was moving out of the kitchen towards the staircase door even as she spoke. So natural did she keep her chatter that Ginger and she passed through the sitting-room and into her bedroom without arousing any comment from the four rummaging amongst the things piled on the table.

Trailing behind the broad-shouldered youth, Alice began to experience little swoops of nervous excitement. Oh, God. Please make him help me, she prayed, please, please, make him understand. Under cover of the protesting squeal the sashcord emitted as Ginger flung up the window, she whispered frantically, 'Ginger. I must talk to you. On your own, son. Can you come back when the others have gone?'

'Eh?' The youth turned from the window, clutching the bottle of milk, and gawped at her.

'Shh! Don't let them hear.' Alice felt sick. So much depended on Ginger grasping the situation before the others became suspicious about the length of time they were absent.

'Come back tonight—alone!' she hissed.

Ginger regarded her warily and Alice was miserably certain that he meant to ignore her request. Taking hold of his sleeve she gave it a tug, and, putting all the heartfelt persuasion she was capable of into the single word, begged intently, 'Please! Oh, please, Ginger. Please.'

CHAPTER 8

Ginger went guiltily back to the others, leaving Alice to make her protracted journey behind him. He hoped no one had heard her frantic whispers. A hasty scan of their faces from beneath lowered brows reassured him. But he came close to giving the game away as relief pushed him into overplaying his hand.

'Huh! Talk about wanting a servant,' he said over-loudly. 'Do this, Ginger. Ginger, do that, and don't let, don't . . .' he floundered, being too slow to substitute an innocent prohibition for the one he'd so nearly given away.

'Don't what?' Paul took up swiftly, his habitual distrust clear in his face.

'Oh, er, I d'know. Don't anythin', you know how she is.' A dull flush ran up under his freckles, and he shuffled his oversized feet, anticipating the tongue-lashing he'd collect if Paul found him out. To his relief his explanation was accepted without further question and he resolved to steer clear of being alone with Alice in the future. He'd got a pretty good thing going here with Paul and the others, he didn't want to mess it all up.

'Right, then.' Paul took the floor and his audience looked towards him expectantly. Keeping an eye on the door Alice could shortly be expected to come through, he said quickly, 'It's a bit of a drag having the old bag getting wise to us, I know. But she don't know it all, and she ain't goin' ter find out, see? Not from any of yer.' His sweeping glance threatened murder for any who dared disobey. 'As long as she don't get out, away from this house, we're okay. So it's up to you lot ter keep an eye on her, make sure she stays put. I can't do everythin' miself.

There's nobody comes here 'cept us and there's nobody ter miss her round here, anyway, so it won't be a hard job.'

'What about her pension and that? If she don't go ter collect it somebody might twig, maybe come round here ter see if she's okay or summat,' Elaine put in before Paul could continue.

'She ain't due for no more pension yet awhile, is she? And I'll think of somethin' before next week, don't worry your fat guts.'

Stung because she had picked out the one weak spot in his plans, Paul glared at the overweight girl. This was his show, his chance to shine as their leader, and he didn't intend to have anyone stealing his thunder.

'Er, when do we stand to collect?' Ginger rubbed a grimy thumb and forefinger together in a meaningful gesture.

'Next week, some time. After Steve sends it through.'

'Next week! But what about all this lot here on this table? There must be summat to come from all this.' Ginger was stung into argument.

'Next week, I tell you,' said Paul fiercely, ready to lash out at anyone fool enough to question his judgment.

Ginger thrust out his lower lip and turned his attention to Elaine. 'Hey, what about givin' us some money, Elaine? You and your Tony should have some left.'

'If we have, we're keepin' it.' Tony sprang to the defence of his hoard.

'No you're bloody well not.' John felt safe now to protest, remembering Paul's rage at Tony's making off with the money, and feeling hopeful of gaining his aid if it came to a fight.

'Well, it's no use you carpin', cos we've stashed it away where you'll never find it. So there.'

John found Tony's jeering reply and his out-thrust tongue just provocation to aim a punch at his head. As always when her brother was threatened, Elaine lurched into the breach.

Coming softly to the door, Alice heard the scuffle begin and decided she'd be safer to stay where she was.

Paul was quite content to let them battle it out between themselves; no sense in getting embroiled in a free-for-all when he could stand on the sidelines and retain his position as leader by merely swiping them all round the ear when they finally ran out of steam; while Ginger, whose bulk ensured he seldom needed to fight, suddenly grew bored with the lot of them and set off, after a casual 'So long, then, Paul. I'll see yer termorrer,' to seek diversion elsewhere.

Leaving the house, he trudged along the derelict streets of the neighbourhood, hands thrust deep into his pockets, head lowered and shoulders hunched against the keen wind, kicking at the rubble strewn around from the demolition currently in progress. The failure of his brain to keep pace with his body's rapid development had set him apart from boys of his own age and he had been something of a loner until Paul came into his life. From the moment they met, both clandestinely sneaking a smoke behind the sports pavilion of the school they so seldom frequented, he had fallen under the younger boy's domination.

'Hey. Where d'yer manage ter get a full pack?' Paul had asked, eyeing the twenty cigarettes Ginger pulled out of his pocket. 'Nick yer Dad's, did yer?'

'Nah. Mrs Maxwell gave me the money. She allus does,' said Ginger, staring in fascination as Paul rolled a makeshift smoke from a cancerous mixture of cinder-tipped dog-ends.

'Mrs Maxwell? Don't she mind if you smoke, then?'

'Don't think she knows. She thinks I spent it on toffees,' said Ginger with a grin.

'Who is she, then? Not yer mam?'

'Nah. She's an old girl that used ter live near us. We moved out, though, 'cos they were pullin' the street down. She wouldn't move. She's still there.'

'Where? Where does she live?'

'Princess Street, near the old stadium. You know, out by the gasworks.'

'I know. Thought that was all flat round there,' said Paul slowly, his eyes narrowed thoughtfully against the acrid smoke from the tobacco stick in his lips.

'Not yet it's not. 'Cos Mrs Maxwell won't move out, see? There's her place and two bits of the houses next door still standin'.'

'How often do you go round there?'

'Ooh, 'bout once or twice a week.'

'And she gives yer money?'

'Sometimes; mostly, really,' said Ginger, wriggling in some embarrassment at the barrage of questions from this boy he'd never met before.

'Do you live round here?' he was asking now as he ground out the stub of his homemade cigarette.

'Yeah, well, not far off. In Ogden Place.'

'I know it. I live in the high-rise just back of there. Look, why don't we team up? Mates, like?'

Ginger gaped at the small, narrow-featured child standing before him. No one had ever offered to be his special friend before, and he could hardly believe he wasn't having his leg pulled. 'Course, he knew the boy could only be about ten or eleven, but even so Ginger was immensely flattered.

'Okay,' he said at last, a broad grin spreading over his homely face. 'I'd like that.'

'Ye'r on, then,' said Paul. 'Now give us one o' them fags.'

For the first few days after that meeting Ginger and Paul met by arrangement on the council waste-tip which lay well outside the town boundary. They would smoke

Ginger's cigarettes and gossip as they rummaged amongst the dirt and refuse, hunting for the odd item of value that might have mistakenly found its way into one of the town's dustbins. In this manner they came to know each other and to develop their friendship, neither of them unduly worried by the fact that they should both have been in school. When Ginger lifted the dirt-encrusted box of about four inches square from amongst the wet ash and potato peelings and shook it experimentally, finding it heavy, it was Paul who snatched it away and stripped the soggy cardboard from the gold powder compact.

'Cor.' Ginger's full, moist lips gaped apart. 'Cor, look at that. Is it real gold?'

'Shouldn't think so, but I bet it's worth a bit all the same.' Paul opened the compact and surveyed his narrow face in the clear mirror inside the lid. He prinked a little, screwing his mouth and eyes in a ferocious grimace before snapping the case shut and dropping it into his pocket.

'Hey! That's mine. I found it.' Ginger made a futile grab as the compact slid from his sight.

'What yer goin' to do with it? Powder yer gob?' Paul gave vent to a howl of laughter, pleased with his own joke.

Ginger grinned, shamefaced, then dissolved into giggles as Paul continued to laugh.

'Look,' said Paul at last, wiping his streaming eyes on the sleeve of his coat, for their laughter had grown almost hysterical, going far beyond what his feeble attempt at humour had called for. 'I'll take it to my mate's, see? He'll buy it off us if it's any good, then we'll split fifty-fifty. Okay?'

'Okay.' Ginger was quite happy with this proposal. 'How much d'yer suppose it'll fetch?'

'Can't say. Depends on whether he can flog it himself. Should be a quid or two, though.'

'Hey, fantastic. Wish we could find some more, it's like buried treasure, ain't it?'

'Well, we don't have to stick to the tip, you know. We could try Woolies or somewhere,' said Paul slowly, his eyes never leaving Ginger's face.

'Woolies?' Ginger's nose wrinkled so hard in enquiry that his freckles ran together in a gold splodge.

'Yeah. Why not? S'easy. They never watch yer much in there. We could make a bomb.'

'What? — Y'mean — yer mean, pinchin'?' asked Ginger, light beginning to dawn.

'Yeah. Like I say, why not?'

'What if they catch yer?'

'They won't. 'N' if they do, you just play it soft, like. Sniffles and tears and promises to be a good boy in future. Get me?'

'Nah. My mam 'ud kill me if she found out.' Ginger kicked at a rusty can, partly ashamed to be the one to cry off.

'She won't. Mine never has and I've nicked plenty,' Paul stated baldly.

'Nah, better not,' said Ginger, sliding his eyes away from Paul's commanding gaze.

'All right then, suit yerself. I didn't know you were a friggin' softie.' Stiff with contempt, the younger boy turned abruptly about and stomped off towards the road.

'Wait. Wait,' Ginger, with his much longer stride, soon overtook the hurrying figure. 'Okay, then. I'm in if you say so,' he offered placatingly.

'Right. C'mon, then.' Anger dismissed, Paul rewarded him with a very rare smile and they set off together towards the shops of the town.

At first Ginger was too scared of being caught out to make an apt pupil in this Fagin-style partnership. Obeying Paul's whispered insistence, he would trail after him around the big stores, watching as the quick, grubby hands gleaned a treasure from fixtures carelessly displaying all manner of wares.

'S'your turn next,' Paul promised, steering Ginger towards a camera display. 'Try and get summat from there.'

Ginger's heart thumped a painful tattoo and the guilty colour rose in his cheeks as he circled the camera stand.

'Go on,' hissed Paul. 'I'll keep conk. Be quick.'

Ginger swallowed desperately, fear bringing a mistiness to his eyes as he reached a blundering hand amongst the gleaming camera lenses. A clattering avalanche ensued and Ginger sprang away, starting into a shambling run. Paul had already disappeared.

'Just a minute.' A female figure blocked Ginger's escape. 'What are you up to?' Accusing eyes probed his sweat-beaded face.

'I . . . I . . .' There was an appealing childishness in the way he lifted his great hands, palms upwards, in helpless loss.

Watching him flounder, his captor was conscious of a wave of pity. He's a mongol, she thought erroneously. Poor soul, he's probably half scared to death. Her face relaxed into a smile.

'Did you knock the cameras over?' she asked solicitously. 'Don't worry, son. I'll soon get someone to put them to rights. Off you go now.' Giving his shoulder a motherly pat, she ushered him on his way.

Ginger could hardly believe his luck. He'd been so scared his legs were still shaking and he stumbled towards one of the store's many exits in unconscious confirmation of the floorwalker's most sympathetic diagnosis of his mental state. Paul was waiting for him as he emerged from the store.

'You bloody great loon. What the hell do yer think yer was doin'?' His slight frame bristled with anger.

Ginger grinned sheepishly, his courage flooding back now he was clear of the store.

'I couldn't help it. They was all too close together,' he complained.

'What did that woman say ter yer?'

'Nothin'. Just said it was all right.'

'All right?' Paul stared at him in disbelief.

'Yeah. C'mon. Let's try somewhere else.' Ginger's newly won courage swept away his previous caution and he was eager now to prove his capabilities in this new game.

Once he got into the way of it, Ginger experienced no further difficulty in matching Paul's expertise as a shoplifter, his simple, homely face providing an unexpected bonus, since few people subjected such bland innocence to a second glance. Soon the sheer amount of stuff they were stealing between them presented its own problems. Paul's friend, Steven, was always ready to buy anything they had, but he was a shifting, shadowy figure, who came and went in his own good time, and the two boys needed somewhere safe to store their hoard until they were able to make a trade with it. That was when Paul took himself to meet Alice.

He made no mention to Ginger of his intended visit. He simply walked around to Princess Street, rapped on Alice's back door, and admitted himself to her home. Alice had stared in surprise at the waiflike figure.

'Why, hello,' she had said, 'and who might you be, then?'

'I'm Paul. You're Mrs Maxwell, aren't you?' Paul had advanced into the sitting-room to stand in front of Alice's chair, and the two of them scrutinized each other carefully before Alice spoke again.

'Yes, I'm Mrs Maxwell right enough, as folks from these parts will no doubt tell you, but I don't remember as how I've ever seen you before.' She experienced no apprehension as the narrow black eyes gazed boldly back into hers, the boy's general air of neglect sweeping away her normal cautious reserve; and her heart went out to him.

'There's some biscuits in the cupboard, son,' she offered, taking him to be as hungry as he looked, 'and there's milk or tea if you'd like some.'

An innocent still when it came to deceit, Ginger was astounded when he in turn arrived to find Paul firmly ensconced at Alice's table, tucking into milk and biscuits.

'Hey! What are you doin' here?' His voice squeaked his surprise.

'What's it look like?' Paul indicated his plate and cup.

'But I didn't know you knew Mrs Maxwell.' Ginger flicked his gaze from Paul to Alice and back again in rapid enquiry.

'Why, I might have known,' said Alice warmly. 'Of course, you two are pals. How else would Paul have got here?' Her acceptance of the boy was now so complete she needed no further explanation. 'Get yourself a plate, lad. We might as well all eat together,' she said to Ginger, who did as he was bid, his slow brain groping with a host of half-formed questions. Paul managed to catch his eye as he slid his legs under the table, and with a savage frown accompanied by a sharp shake of the head managed to prevent Ginger from actually voicing any of them.

'D'yer live here all by yerself?' Paul enquired politely of Alice, keeping a fierce eye on Ginger.

'That's right, lad. I do. Have done ever since my Sid passed away.'

'What about next door, nobody live there?'

'Not now, no. Nobody left in this street now but me.'

'Bet yer get all them council gits comin' round all the time, don't yer?'

'Not on your life,' Alice replied firmly. 'They mostly know to leave me alone by now.'

Paul gave a satisfied smile.

'Well, thanks fer the biscuits,' he said, pushing back his chair. 'Me'n' Ginger's got ter go now.'

'Eh?' Ginger blinked at him, a biscuit halfway to his mouth.

'C'mon,' Paul hissed as he passed by his chair. Turning

at the door he smiled soulfully at Alice. 'Tarrah, then, Mrs Maxwell. I'll come and see yer again.'

'Yes, do, lad,' she said, smiling affably at the two boys, 'and don't leave it too long, now.'

Once they were out in the back yard Ginger burst into speech. 'Why didn't yer say yer was comin'? How did yer know where ter come? What did —'

'Hang on. Hang on.' Paul steered his spluttering companion across the back yard and round the corner of the lavatory wall, out of sight of the window by Alice's chair. 'I didn't say owt because I didn't want yer ter tell her,' he said. 'I wanted ter come and see the setup fer myself.'

'Setup. What setup?' Ginger was lost.

'This setup, stupid. I'm thinkin' of using the house next door ter keep all our stuff in, see?'

'What for?' Ginger was amazed at this revelation.

'What d'yer think for? We've got ter keep it somewhere. An' there's as good a place as any. No snoopers. No chance the place'll get pulled down with the old girl sittin' tight, an' we'll have a good excuse fer comin' here regular — ter visit her, like. Now do yer see?' Paul asked with heavy patience.

'Why don't we just ask Mrs Maxwell ter let us stick the stuff in her upstairs rooms? She never uses 'em now.'

'Don't be more stupid than you can help. What are we supposed ter tell her we're doin' with it? Keepin' a bloody shop? C'mon, let's go round the front, then there's no chance she'll spot us.' Paul led the way into the street along the narrow entry that had once been the only access to the rear of the long row of terraced houses.

CHAPTER 9

Paul and Ginger turned into the street at the entry end, passed by Alice's front window and the boarded square in the wall of the neighbouring house, then turned again to enter the half-demolished shell. The galvanized wire mesh erected to keep vagrants away was already prised open, giving access in several places to the ground-floor rooms. The two boys wriggled through the larger of the holes and made their way over fallen plaster and brick rubble to mount the stairs leading to the upper rooms.

'S'like a doll's house, this is.' Ginger grinned as he looked around one of the rooms, open now along its entire length to the force of the elements.

'Yeah. Not much good ter us, though, is it?' Paul glanced around in disgust. 'I never realized there was so much of it gone. Can't leave the stuff here; it'd get all wet and grotty, that's if it didn't get pinched.'

'We could shove it up against here.' Ginger crossed to the chimney wall where the old chimneybreast formed a sheltered alcove. This wall backed on to Alice's former bedroom, the two houses sharing the common chimney flue.

'Nah. Somebody might come up here and find it.'

'Well, then, why can't we just ask Mrs Maxwell, like I said?'

'For cryin' out loud. Won't you ever give up? No, I told yer. And no, I meant. We'll just have ter think of somewhere else.' Paul aimed a disgruntled punch at the wall and the ageing plaster gave under his fist, bringing huge chunks away from the brickwork. 'Hey, just a minute, though. What if we could make a hole in this wall through ter next door? That'd be okay. We could come in and out without her knowin' and stash things away right over her head.' As he spoke, Paul was prodding and poking at the exposed bricks; there was a trickle of dust and a series of gaps began to appear as the ancient cement ran from between the bricks. 'C'mon, Ginger. Don't just stand there. Come and give us a hand.'

Ginger shrugged helplessly. His companion's mind moved too swiftly for him to hope to keep up.

In spite of the apparently crumbling state of the old wall, they had to return with a hammer and chisel, borrowed without permission from Ginger's dad, before they were able to make an opening large enough for them to step through with ease. They had worked as quietly as possible, lifting the bricks and rubble away from the widening gap to prevent anything falling with a clatter that might alarm Alice, who sat below in happy ignorance of their activities.

'That'll do, I think,' Paul said at last, brushing brickdust and plaster from his clothing. 'Now let's see what's what.' He disappeared through the hole into Alice's side of the wall. Ginger hastened to follow.

'Careful how you step,' Paul cautioned. 'Don't make your usual bloody row.'

The room was damp and musty; only an old wardrobe, its oak veneer peeling in long bright strips, remained of the 'modern' utility suite Alice had so proudly purchased to furnish this bedroom after the war.

'Yeah, this'll do nicely,' said Paul, gazing around. 'An' if we take the door off that,' he nodded towards the wardrobe, 'we can use it ter cover the hole we've made in the wall.'

'What d'yer want ter do that for?' asked Ginger, who could see no sensible reason for making any extra effort. 'Ain't nobody goin' ter look up here.'

'Pays ter be safe. 'Sides, it'll keep birds and cats an' things out,' came the answer in a tone that left no room for argument.

Having a warehouse for his wildly assorted gains made
Paul ambitious, and it wasn't long before he'd recruited
Elaine, Tony and John into his service. Their inclusion
was a happy circumstance for Ginger, since he was never
very successful at keeping secrets, and they helped enor-
mously when it came to deceiving Alice over the use being
made of her property. What he couldn't quite figure out,
in spite of all Paul's attempted explanations, was why he
now had less of a share in their joint profits than he'd had
previously.

'S'easy,' Paul had declared. 'I get half, the kids get a
quid apiece, an' you get the rest. What's so hard about
that?'

'Well, didn't I used to get more? I mean, when there
was just you and me.'

'Ah, but we've got ter give the kids their dues, don't
forget.'

'Ye-es, I s'pose so.' Ginger had remained unconvinced,
but lacked the wit to argue the matter further. The only
trouble was, now that he had a girl-friend he found he
had a much greater need of money than ever.

It was this lack of funds that was responsible for the worried crease on Ginger's brow as he emerged from the
clearance area and turned towards the sprawling council
estate where his own family and most of their former
neighbours had been rehoused. He was meeting his girl
this evening and she would expect him to take her to the
disco, or maybe up to the pub. Either way, it was Ginger
who would be expected to pay for their entertainment
and he hadn't a bean. A hefty kick at an empty tin rolling
along the litter-strewn pavement helped relieve his feelings and he arrived at a possible conclusion to his
problem; he would ask their Janice. She was his sister,
and always good for the odd quid or two since she started
work. And anyway, he would promise to pay her back. He

shouldered his way through the front door of his home
and burst into the room where his father sprawled in an
easy chair, his eyes glued to a flickering television set.

'Where's our Janice?' he asked, casting a searching
glance round the room.

'Gone out,' his father answered without looking up
from the set.

'Gone out where?' There came no answer, so Ginger
tried again. 'Eh? Dad! Gone out where?'

'How should I know? Shoppin', I expect.' He leaned
closer to the television set, intent on the football match in
progress.

'Aw, I wanted ter see her.' Ginger began to grumble
before his attention was captured by the miniature figures
running across the screen. It wasn't until an attempted
goal-scoring run by the favourites was brought to a halt
by a foul from the opposing striker that his thoughts
swung back to his immediate problem.

'Couldn't lend me some money, Dad, could yer?' he
asked hopefully.

'No, I bloody well couldn't. D'yer think I'm made of it,
or summat? You've had yer pocket money this week, be
satisfied with that, and get out of the road of the telly, I'm
tryin' ter watch this game.'

With a sigh of disgust Ginger flung himself into a chair
and chewed impatiently at his fingernails while he waited
for his sister to come home.

It was dark, with the early nights of November, before
the click of the front garden gate announced the arrival
of Janice and her mother. Ginger sprang from his chair
and was at the door to meet them, scarcely giving them
time to get into the house before he began his request.

'Sorry, Trevor. I'm just as skint as you are now,' Janice
indicated her parcels as she removed her outdoor coat
and rubbed her chilled hands together.

'Brr, it's freezing out there. You'd be better off staying

in tonight, anyway.'

'I've got ter go out. I've made arrangements. Aw, Janice, come on, yer must have a couple of quid yer can spare.'

'No, I haven't, honestly. Why don't you ask Mum?'

'Nah, you know what she'll say.' Ginger gazed mournfully at his mother, who had been listening to the interchange between brother and sister as she too removed her topcoat.

'It's no good you giving me the sad eye,' she said, exchanging a conspiratorial smile with her daughter. 'I've just spent all my spare cash on a new pair of shoes for your Dad, but there's kippers for tea and doughnuts to follow, so that should make you feel better.'

'I haven't got time for tea. I tell you I've got to go out.' Ginger snatched the front door open, disappointment making him angry. 'Yer can save it fer me supper,' he shouted as he marched out of the house.

'Trevor! Trevor, just you come back here.' His mother called vainly after his departing figure before turning back into the house with a sigh. 'I don't know what's got into that lad lately,' she told her daughter, who gave a negligent shrug.

'Oh, he's growing up, I expect, getting manny. They all do at his age,' she said fondly, as if it were she who was mother to them both. 'Come on, let's go and show Dad his new shoes, don't let our Trev bother you.'

Ginger was indeed growing up, and experiencing all the trauma of an adolescent's first love. Nothing had prepared this simple-minded lad for the thrill and the hurt and the wonder he found in the company of his girl. She awoke needs and urges in him he was at a loss to understand, and could only express by showering her with every trinket and token her eyes fell upon. Tongue-tied and slow-witted, he relied upon making a splash with his money to woo her and keep her ever close to his side.

There were others who looked for a chance with his Freda, he was certain of that, but they'd never get it, not while he could swagger up to the disco with his pockets stuffed with cash. The big hands closed convulsively at the thought and Ginger checked his aimless footsteps as his fingers encountered nothing but air. He was beginning to get desperate. He just had to get some money from somewhere.

Slouching into a deserted bus shelter, he scratched industriously at its painted surface while he attempted to think. If only those two greedy sods, Tony and Elaine, hadn't collared all of Ma's money, he'd be okay. She'd always seen him right in the past, had old Ma. The memory of Alice's whispered plea came into his mind. 'Come back tonight. After the others have gone,' she'd asked him. Well, and why not? P'raps she'd got a bit more tucked away somewhere. Anyway, it was worth a try. Better than standin' about here gettin' froze. Stuffing his hands into his pockets, Ginger set off at a brisk pace towards Alice's home.

It had seemed almost a lifetime to Alice before the children went, leaving her undisturbed to wait on the outcome of her plea to Ginger.

Paul, being the last to go, had followed her into her bedroom and removed her walking-frame.

'You'll have ter stop here now till one of us gets here termorrer,' he told her, and she'd made no protest, merely stared after him sadly as he slid out of the door. Fully dressed, she leaned back on her pillows and tried to settle with patience to await Ginger's coming, refusing to let herself even consider the possibility that he might not turn up. 'He has to come. He has to,' she chanted softly, as if by her will alone she could make him appear. Both her strength and her faith in his coming were rubbed to a wafer before the door was blessedly opened to admit the redheaded boy.

'Thank God!' she whispered, struggling to an upright position.

'What did yer want me for, Ma? You'll have ter tell me quick. I can't hang about in case Paul comes back.' Ginger hung in the doorway as if ready for instant flight.

'No! You can't go again. Not without me, Ginger.' Panic swept away her resolve to use reasoned persuasion on the lad and her voice was shrill, betraying her fear.

'They'll be the death of me, don't you see? They'll kill me between them.' Her clutching hand reached towards him in frantic appeal.

Alarm swept Ginger's features and he backed hastily away.

'Hey . . . I . . . look, I've got ter go.' God! he hadn't bargained for this. Paul 'ud kill him if he upset all his plans. Only his pressing need of a handout kept him from departing with all speed.

'No, please.' Alice made a desperate bid to get herself under control. 'Don't go, Ginger, I'm sorry I shrieked at you.'

Ginger continued his wary regard, and she hurriedly sought to allay his fears.

'I'm old, very old, lad. That's all it is. I can't be doing with all this excitement. The others can't seem to understand that, but you can. You're older than them, got more sense.'

Alice had struck the right note. Ginger began to relax, enjoying her flattery.

'Now I know you're using my upstairs rooms as a store place, and I don't mind about that,' Alice went on soothingly, 'but I can't be kept cooped up like I am. I need to be able to get about a bit, stretch my legs, like. And I'll have to get down to the shops come Thursday, for my pension and that.' She watched Ginger anxiously, afraid to rush on too fast in case she scared him again.

'Couldn't you and your young lady get rid of the others

one afternoon,' she ventured, 'say, tomorrow? Then the three of us could maybe take a taxi into town and have a look round the shops. Maybe have lunch or something in a café,' she added coaxingly. 'What do you say, lad?' She held her breath as she waited to see the effect of her words.

'Nah, can't. Paul wouldn't let us,' he said at last.

'But he needn't know. We'd be back before he found out, and I bet your young lady isn't frightened of him, anyway.' Alice added her masterstroke, praying the boy's vanity would work in her favour.

'Pooh, Freda's not afraid of nothing,' he bragged, falling into the trap. 'She'd soon show him where to get off.'

'Well, then, why don't we do it? We could have a lovely time. I'll draw some money out of the Post Office and we'll really paint the town,' Alice urged.

'Don't suppose you've got the odd quid on you now, have you, Ma?" Ginger was reminded of the real purpose of his visit.

'Nay, I'm sorry, lad. I haven't. But you can have all you want if you can get me into town.'

Ginger pondered the situation, then decided it was the best he could hope for. He had no real hope of gaining any money elsewhere, and perhaps, if he was to promise Freda a day out tomorrow, she wouldn't be too mad at him for not taking her anywhere tonight.

'Well, okay, then,' he said at last. 'I'll tell Freda ternight. Only, just you be ready termorrer, won't yer?'

'Oh, I will, lad. I will.' Alice beamed at him with renewed vigour.

'Right, then. I'd better go now. Say nowt ter the others, and don't forget — be ready.'

Relief brought a lump to Alice's throat, making reply impossible as Ginger left the room. The ring of his footsteps through the entry told her when he gained the street, and she heaved a quivering sigh. 'May God forgive

me for telling such lies,' she said with feeling, finally daring to uncross her fingers. Even given the aid of her
walking-frame Alice knew it would be impossible for her
to get into town alone, but if Ginger and his girl would
help her get as far as the nearest telephone box she would
manage the rest for herself. She eased herself back on her
pillows and busied her mind with her plans. She realized
that she was banking heavily on the good nature of an
unknown girl, and much would depend on the sort of per-
son she was. Thinking about it carefully, Alice guessed
Freda would be somewhere about Ginger's own age,
around fourteen or fifteen, say. Which should mean she
was old enough to understand the trouble Alice was in.
Girls have more gumption than lads when it came to that
sort of thing, Alice told herself firmly.

Why, given a bit of good luck, she thought with a rising
optimism, once I've explained to the girl just what has
been going on here I probably won't need to do any more,
she will take over and do all that's necessary. But if not,
then I'll do what I think best. Maybe telephone the
welfare people and ask to be taken in. Yes, that would be
best. I'll speak to them and tell them I've changed my
mind about going to live in an old folks' place. I won't
bother the police, no sense in getting the youngsters into
any bother. They are not to blame for all this, they don't
really know how cruel they're being, nor how silly with
their 'nicking' things. And once I get out of here they'll
pull this old place down pretty quick, so they won't be
able to come hiding upstairs in the night and frightening
folks half to death.

Easing herself round on the bed, trying to find some
relief from the ache in her joints, Alice went over her pro-
posed plan of escape again and again. She couldn't afford
to make any mistake, this might well prove to be her last
chance. If only she had some idea what Freda was like.
Would she be the sort that would be willing to help? And

for nothing? Because all that twaddle she had fed to Ginger about drawing money out of the Post Office was simply that; twaddle. She hadn't a penny piece to her name now, not until next pension day. Thinking about her pension brought Ron to mind. He would help if only he knew. Of course he would. Why had she never thought about him before? Alice felt a surge of relief. What a fool she'd been not to have reckoned on him. She would be far better phoning him than the welfare, wouldn't she? 'Specially since she was going to have to ask him to pay for the 'phone call.

Alice wasn't at all certain how to go about that part of it. She knew that it was possible to make a 'phone work without putting any money into the box but she didn't know exactly how it was done. 'I'll just ask the girl,' she said softly, trying to bolster her flagging confidence. 'She'll tell me what to do, I know.' And then, when she got hold of Ron she'd tell him to come at once to the 'phone-box in his taxi and get her. She did spare a brief thought at this point to merely waiting until next Thursday when Ron was due to call for her here at her home, but some inner voice warned her that would be too late. No, she had to get away as soon as possible, while she still had the strength.

What she was to do with herself once she was safely out of reach of the children became Alice's next concern.

In spite of everything she was still not resigned to spending the rest of her days as an inmate of some institution. Perhaps Ron would be able to suggest something, she thought hopefully. Or maybe . . . maybe . . . Here a swift leaping thrill of excitement caught at her throat, making her gasp and choke over her next breath. *Maybe she could go out to Australia to her Georgie.* The enormity of the thought was overwhelming. Why had she never had that idea before? What absolute stupidity, hanging about here in this crumbling old house when she might have been out in the sunshine of a brave new land with her boy and his children.

Making herself consider the idea from all aspects, Alice had first to admit that Georgie had never once asked her to join him and his family. But that was only because he thought she was too firmly settled where she was, she told herself. Why, he would be just as pleased as Punch when she wrote to tell him she was going to travel out to him. Blithely lost in her eager anticipation of seeing not only her son but also her unknown daughter-in-law and her grandchildren, Alice completely lost sight of the necessity of finding the money to pay for her fare. That was a consideration furthermost from her mind.

So eager was she now to see that part of her scheme put into motion, she found herself too restless to sleep. Silly old fool, she chided herself almost happily as she tossed and turned, calling fresh agony from her creaking joints. Fancy getting worked up like this at your age, you ought to know better.

The hours of darkness crept past and the faint light of breaking day streaked the lowering sky before the wild beat of her heart steadied and her twitching limbs began to relax.

Her last conscious thought before sleep claimed her was a rather determined resolve to make sure she had plenty of sea-sickness pills before ever she set foot on board that outgoing ship. Wouldn't do for her to arrive on Georgie's doorstep like some ailing dependent, now, would it?

CHAPTER 10

It was Paul himself who appeared early the next morning, slouching round the door of her bedroom before she was properly awake. She blinked at him, unable to think who he was or why he was there. Still caught in the dredges of sleep, she struggled to sit up, her movements hampered by her crumpled woollen dress.

As she looked down on it, wondering how she came to be in her bed fully dressed, she found herself half afraid to make a guess at the reason.

It must be Sid, was her first heartsick thought. He must be ill again, please God he wasn't in pain. The days and nights she had spent sitting by his bed, snatching the odd hour of sleep, too spent to remove her clothing, crowded back into her memory. And with them the fresh pain of bereavement. Slow tears slid down her cheeks.

'What yer bawlin' about? I ain't even spoke ter yer yet.' Contempt loaded Paul's voice.

Alice had forgotten his presence and she gave a start of surprise as he spoke. Unable to see through her tears, she asked wonderingly. 'W-who is it? Who is there?' Could it . . . could it possibly . . . was it her Georgie?

'It's me, stupid. Me. Paul.'

'Paul?' Disappointment crushed her timid hope but the name brought no recognition.

'Oh, for crying out loud. Here!' Her walking-frame was hurled towards the bed. 'And don't take all day about it, neither. I could do with some breakfast.' The slight figure slid away round the door.

Something in the furtive manner of movement brought Alice crashing back to the present. Paul! Oh no! What was he doing here? He didn't usually come here till later, much later. And today she had been praying he would stay away altogether. Was he here because he had guessed her arrangement with Ginger? Swift terror clutched her at the thought. But no, hadn't he said something about breakfast? In that case she had not better lie there any longer, just in case he got angry.

Anxious now to learn the reason for his early visit and eager to do all she could to placate him and speed him on his way, she scrambled painfully from the bed. She entered her sitting-room to find him sprawled comfortably in a chair drawn up to the gas fire. Normally, she would have a wash and do what she could to make herself tidy before thinking of starting the day, but circumstances were far from normal. And what did her appearance matter, she asked herself, if a little neglect meant a quick escape from the menace of those slitted eyes?

'What would you like for your breakfast, then?' She was apprehensive of his reply, knowing there was very little in her larder that would appeal to him.

'How about egg on toast?'

Alice felt a surge of relief; that should be easy enough. Eggs she did have. Now what about bread? The loaf she'd bought when she went into town had hardly been touched, it was stale of course, but that wouldn't matter for toast. She prepared the meal as quickly as she could, forcing her limbs to a speed almost forgotten in her desire to keep the boy from losing his patience.

'There you are,' she laid the plate at his elbow and handed him a knife and fork.

'What about something to drink?' He scowled at her, his cheeks stuffed with food.

'Oh. Oh, I forgot. I'll just get the milk.' Alice made the laborious journey across the room, past the staircase, and in through the front room to the window. Sliding the lower pane up with an ease born of long practice, she lifted the milk from the sill. It's a good job Ginger didn't see that, she thought, ruefully remembering her pretended difficulties of the day before, invented to get him into the room and away from the others. If only she could think of something equally effective to get rid of Paul before Freda and Ginger should come.

A resounding belch informed her that Paul had cleared his plate and was waiting for his coffee. A splash or two spilled as she carried it from the kitchen to the table; she was unused to managing her frame while holding a cup and saucer. She usually dispensed with the saucer when making a drink for herself, but something warned her not to do so in this instance. Paul watched her difficulties with detached amusement, making no effort to rise and take the cup from her. Alice waited until he'd taken an overloud slurp of its contents before she ventured to ask the question uppermost in her mind.

'What, er, what brings you around so early?' She strove to keep her voice casual.

'I can come when I want, can't I? Or do I have ter clock in or summat?'

'Oh, no, no.' Alice hastened to soothe him. 'I just thought it was a bit unusual to see you here ahead of the others, that's all.'

'Well, you'd better get used to it, Ma, because they're back at school termorrer, and that leaves only me.' There was a certain cruel satisfaction in the look he turned on Alice that made an apprehensive shudder run down her spine.

'School? . . . tomorrow?' she faltered. 'What . . . what day is today, then?'

'Blimey! Are you goin' potty? Don't yer even know what day it is?'

'I . . . I get a bit mixed up sometimes. Specially now I don't have the wireless —' her voice trailed guiltily away as she recalled that it was Paul's fault her set was now useless. If he thought she was rebuking him by deliberately bringing her loss to his notice, he might turn nasty. Fortunately, he was so eager to prove her a fool that he didn't notice her lapse.

'What day d'yer think it is, Ma? Mondy? Wensdy? Come on, what day d'yer think?'

'I don't know, Paul, I'm sure.' She watched him anxiously. Was he going to tell her?

'It's Sunday. That's why the kids aren't here—they've all gone to Sunday School.' He gave a hoot of laughter over this shaft of wit, knowing full well none of them had ever set foot inside a church since the day they were christened. If they ever had been.

'Sunday.' Alice felt sick. Sunday. The shops were all closed, the post office and everywhere, even Ginger would know that. So he wouldn't come. She was trapped here for another twenty-four hours at least. But was there any chance he would come after that? Dear God, what a senile old fool she'd become. Her one chance of escape lost through her own foolish stupidity.

Depressed and discouraged by the collapse of her plans Alice stared blankly out of the window. The bleak wintry outlook fitted well with her mood. From here she could see the leafless boughs of the sooty old lilac, pencilled coldly against the leaden sky. Grey, cheerless November bringing yet another year towards its close. She felt a growing affinity with the dead brown earth. As she stared, a pert beady-eyed robin flew from the lilac to perch on the corner of the lavatory roof. Cocking his head to peer inquisitively into the cracks and crevices between the bricks, he hopped brightly along. Suddenly, the red flag of courage he wore at his breast found an answering spark in Alice's heart. Courage, that was the way, she told herself. No use giving up at the first little setback. She turned resolutely back to face the room and found Paul regarding her closely through the cigarette smoke he expelled through his nostrils.

'I must get myself washed and changed,' she informed him, refusing to be cowed by his stare. 'I've not had these clothes off my back since I don't know when. It's time I livened my ideas up a bit.'

The boy continued to watch her, saying nothing.

'I'm going to go into the kitchen and have a strip wash.' Alice longed to ask him to allow her some privacy but lacked the nerve in the face of his stare. She looked at him doubtfully, then, remembering her resolve, began to make her way towards her bedroom, intent on collecting some clean clothes. As she reached the door he tossed the end of his cigarette towards the gas fire and stood up.

'How long has the kitchen been on that side of the house?' he asked with heavy sarcasm.

'I have to get my clean clothes.' Alice indicated the bedroom door and looked appealingly for his permission.

'Don't take all bloody day, then, I want to go out,' he snapped.

Despite the harsh reply Alice felt a quick lift of her spirits. If he was going out, maybe there was still a chance she could do something to get herself out and away. She selected a fresh set of underwear in a mood bordering on jubilation, then, hanging the fleecy undergarments over the rail of her walking-frame, she pulled open the door of the wardrobe and selected a warm skirt and top. No sense in being unprepared, if she did manage to get out she would need to be warmly dressed. Transporting everything to the kitchen was a tedious business and only accomplished with patience and care, but she was ready at last to begin her ablutions. She hesitated before filling the enamel bowl with warm water. Dare she ask Paul not to come through for a while? The thought of removing her clothing while he was still in her house and might even come into the room where she was, caused her to pause in embarrassed consternation. As she dithered, torn between her desire to make herself clean and tidy and her fear of being caught half-naked, Paul flung back the door and strode into the room.

'I'm going out now, Ma. And I'm takin' yer legs.' He said pulling her frame towards him. 'You won't be goin' far without this.'

'But—but I need it.' Alice clung desperately to the edge of the sink for support. 'You can't leave me here like this, lad. You can't.' Her dread of falling, coupled with this new blow to her optimistic hopes of escape, made the prospect of losing the frame doubly unbearable. She bit hard on her lip to keep back the tears of fear and dismay. The boy remained apparently unmoved by the utter helplessness of her position; he tossed the frame behind him into the sitting-room and turned a gaze of narrow-eyed assessment towards Alice's quivering form. Her knees were beginning to sag beneath her and the terror she felt was very evident as she cried in distress 'No, Paul. Please. Dear God, can't you see I'm going to fall?'

Paul disappeared into the sitting-room and returned with a straight-backed dining-chair which he shoved towards her. 'Here, then. You can sit on this till I get back.' He waited only to see her reach out towards his offering before he slipped round the outer door, and Alice heard him lock it behind him as she transferred her weight to the chair.

It needed all the grit she could muster to make herself go on with her toilet. 'There is one thing about it,' she said aloud, in an effort to buoy up her flagging spirits, 'at least you're sure of a bit of privacy now.' Sitting on the chair she soaped her upper body, laving her neck and shoulders with a piece of old sheet she used as a flannel. There, that was better—nothing like a good wash to make a new woman out of you. A trickle of water ran down her back, raising gooseflesh along her warm skin. Brrr, that was the only trouble with these half-and-half baths. What she wouldn't give for a really good soak in hot soapy water.

The old zinc bath, now, that was really a treat. Steaming on the hearthrug in front of the fire. What could be more comfy than that? Friday nights had always been bath nights when she was a girl. Her Dad would carry the bath in, and Mam would fill it from the boiler at the side of the fire. Then in they would go, two by two, a child at each end regardless of sex until they had all been given a feckling. Then up to bed they went while Mam and Dad used the last of the water before carrying the bath out between them to be tipped down the drain in the winter or left to go cold ready to put on the garden the rest of the year. She and Sid had done just the same, scrubbing the boys before scrubbing each other. It wasn't the same, somehow, washing your own back; how could you be sure it was clean?

She was hardly dressed in her clean clothes before the key was turned in the lock and Paul burst into the kitchen. Thrusting a newspaper-wrapped bundle towards her, a rare grin lighting his face, he spoke even as he turned to leave again.

'Here, cook this fer dinner, and I'll want chips with mine.' The door was closing behind him.

'What? What is it? Hey, just a minute.' Too late; the lock clicked, leaving Alice gingerly poking the package and listening to his footsteps fading away down the entry. The newspaper parted under Alice's fingers to reveal bloodied white paper beneath. She laid this on the draining-board and twitched at the corner. 'Steak. Good heavens, there's pounds of it,' astonishment made her exclaim aloud. She couldn't remember when she'd last seen as much meat, outside of a butcher's, that is. But what was she to do with it? Surely Paul couldn't mean her to cook it all, there was enough to feed an army. Perhaps she'd better wait until he came back. Not that she had very much choice, she realized with a jolt, he still hadn't returned her walking-frame.

Sitting on the straight-backed chair, eyeing the steak, Alice pondered the possibility of getting about without the aid of her frame. If only there was some way she could manage without it, then she might even get away yet.

'If I could just get myself through the front door and into the street,' she breathed. They could hardly drag her kicking and screaming back indoors, could they? There were very few passers-by now the houses were gone, but Alice was prepared to take a chance on catching the odd wanderer. Her heart thumping rapidly, she began to plan how it might be achieved.

Taking a grip on the edge of the kitchen sink, she pulled herself to her feet. Propped against the chipped porcelain, she viewed the chair thoughtfully before releasing her grip to grope towards it with one hand. If she could turn it about and use it in the way she used her frame, working it forwards by tilting it from one leg to the other, the back would be high enough to keep her upright. A wild spiral of hope began in her stomach as the chair rocked towards her and she managed to catch hold of the back. If only. Oh, if only. With a desperate lurch she let go of the sink, trusting herself to the uncertain support of the chair.

For a few dizzy moments she thought it would work. Inch by inch she worked the chair forwards, shuffling along in its wake. Slowly she traversed the length of the kitchen, a breathless excitement clutching her throat. She could do it. It was going to work. Now she was free. So great was her relief she was unable to accept that she had come to a halt on the threshold of the sitting-room. As the bitter truth dawned she tugged frantically at the chair-back. It had to go through. It just had to. Almost in tears, she was forced to acknowledge defeat. She simply hadn't enough strength to manoeuvre the chair across the carpeted floor. There, in the kitchen, over the worn flags, it had been hard enough. But here, with carpet fibre clutching tenaciously at the rough ends of the chair-legs, it was, for Alice, impossible.

Too despondent to eat, she risked firing Paul's uncertain temper by her apparent lack of gratitude when he pressed her to share the steak. Luckily, his outing, whatever it was, had put him in a very good humour, and she escaped retribution. The meal over, she hobbled around, clearing away and washing up, spinning the task out rather longer than necessary. The afternoon stretched endlessly before her, and the prospect of spending it under Paul's unwavering gaze was not at all pleasant. Not for the first time she felt a pang of regret that the need to economize had forced her to cancel the newspapers. She could have hidden behind one of those big Sunday spreads quite safely, and it would have helped while away the hours.

'Fancy a game of cards?' The question, asked in a friendly tone, took her completely by surprise.

'I . . . I, Yes. Yes, if you like, Paul. What shall we play?'

'Strip poker.'

'Pardon?'

' 'S'all right, I'm only joking,' he said with crushing disdain, running a disparaging eye over her shrunken frame. 'C'mon, let's play crib.' The cards flew through his fingers as he shuffled and dealt out their hands.

Making her play and pegging up the scores, Alice began to lose some of her recently induced fear of her opponent. Was it possible, she questioned herself, that he was after all just a normal, rather thoughtless boy, and she an over-sensitive neurotic old woman? She risked a quick glance at the boy's narrow face. His gaze was concentrated on the fan of cards he held. The hard lines etched from his nose to the corners of his mouth were softened as he considered the run of play. Alice was reassured.

They played on, and as Paul continued pleasant, Alice relaxed further. Her guard lowered, she forgot herself so far as to win the next two games. No sign of petulance crossed the boy's face as she moved her peg over the last few holes and confirmed the score. Scooping up the cards, he glanced briefly towards the darkening window before he rose and stretched.

'That's it, Ma. We've played enough fer today,' he said.

'Oh; oh, I was just enjoying myself, son.' Alice smiled up at him, completely disarmed.

'Yeah, I'll just bet you was.' His lip curled in a sneer as he looked down at her.

Stiff from long sitting, Alice struggled to rise from her seat by the table.

'Stay where you are,' he ordered. 'I can see myself out.'

Taken up with the difficulties of getting her limbs mobile, Alice had completely missed the change in his manner, and she chuckled as she explained.

'Eh, lad. I wasn't thinking of showing you out. I'm in need of a trip up the yard, that's all.'

'And I said stay where you are.' This time there was no mistaking his tone of command. She froze in the ungainly posture of half-rising, prickles of trepidation creeping over her flesh. A sharp thrust knocked her back to the chair.

'Your little trip will just have to wait, won't it, Ma? You've been gettin' a bit out of hand.'

Terrified of provoking him further, Alice closed her eyes and sat still. A sharp click, followed by a plunge into greater darkness, warned her the light had been turned out. Stifling a cry of protest, she gripped the seat of the chair for support and risked a swift glance round the room. Paul's dark shape passed in front of the fire before a soft 'plop' from the gas testified that too had been doused.

A series of rattles and bangs followed. Then the back door was wrenched open and a clatter of metal rang from beneath the window as her walking-frame was thrown out into the yard.

'Goodnight, Ma. Pleasant dreams.' His voice was sarcastically sweet. Then the back door crashed to, and the scrape of the lock shooting home told Alice he was gone. Treading lightly on the balls of his feet, the boy emerged from the entry end and sped silently across the demolition area towards the lights of town. He considered he'd had a pretty good day. Filching the steak from under his mam's nose had given him quite a kick, her bloke had thought himself really something when he'd brought it home. Well, let him try finding it now. The thin lips twisted into the nearest they ever got to a smile as he pictured the anger his theft would arouse. Serve 'em right, was his triumphant thought. Piggin' themselves on steak while he, Paul, was left more often than not to scrounge whatever he could amongst the half-empty packets and tins tossed in the cupboards of the flat.

His gleeful thoughts turned from contemplating his home situation to his recently completed mastery over Alice. It didn't lessen his enjoyment of the situation, nor reduce the boost it gave to his ego, to acknowledge that his opponent was a weakened old woman and scarcely a worthy match for his youthful vigour. He enjoyed being the one to dish out the orders, no matter who they were dished out to, and now he could do that all right.

'Crack the whip and see them jump,' one of his mam's blokes used to tell him, and Paul was nothing loath to follow this maxim. Didn't he have the others all waiting on him to tell 'em what to do next? And the old girl? Shit-scared of him, wasn't she? The narrow chest swelled with thoughts of his own importance.

Coming to the busy main road, Paul paused and changed his swift pace for a casual strolling gait. Assuming an air of listless boredom, he passed along the brightly lit road, pausing now and again to stare into some shop window. Here his air of disinterest was hard to maintain, since he made a point of keeping himself fully up to date with the prices they displayed. How else was he to know if he was being ripped off by the guy he sold his stuff to?

Taking the next turn on his left, Paul soon left the shops behind and came to the side entrance of the public

house where he'd arranged to meet Steve. Sliding round
the door, he gained entrance to the dimly lit smoke-room.
There were no customers so early in the evening, a state
he had relied on when making his arrangements. He
couldn't afford to be seen by a room full of nosy people
who might later point the finger at him.

He could hear a babble of voices coming from the
adjoining lounge bar, and he heard what he guessed to be
the landlord's voice giving someone a cheery greeting. So
quickly did he cross the room and regain his place by the
door, it seemed as though the fistful of cigarette packets
he'd snatched from the fixture behind the bar had sprung
into his hands by magic. Stuffing them into his pockets,
he shot a swift glance around the empty plush seating
before backing out of the door into the street.

'Gotcha!' A pair of arms closed around his bony chest.
With a quick downward kick he raked the heel of his shoe
down his captor's shin.

'Hey, you soft sod. It's me.' The arms released him with
a forward push.

Paul whipped around to find himself face to face with
Steve. 'You stupid bastard. Whatcha go an' do that for?'
Spittle accompanied the words over his grimacing lips, so
great had been his shock.

'Okay, okay. So now we're quits.' Steve, a man of
greasy appearance in spite of the flashy rings adorning his
chubby hands, bent to rub his shin. 'My God,' he said
with feeling, 'you ain't half a nervy little bugger.'

CHAPTER 11

So that was it, was it? Alice thought grimly. She was supposed to sit here in the cold and the dark until morning.
Well, she might have been too shocked and hurt to stand
up for herself when all this began, but she'd learned more

sense since then, she told herself firmly. As her eyes grew more accustomed to the dark, so her fighting spirit returned and she began to weigh up her situation.

She was sitting on a chair identical to the one she had been trying to use as a walking-frame earlier that day; her high-seated armchair stood further back, near the window. She judged the table to be close enough for her to use it as a support, and the fireplace was just to her right. Now, could she get to her feet with the aid of the table, then use the back of her chair as a prop while she reached for the mantel? The first stage in her plan gave her no problem, and she stood erect with both hands flat on the table while she gained her sense of balance.

'Oh, what a sin it is to be old,' she told the silent room, swaying slightly as her weakened legs failed to take up her weight. Then, clenching her teeth against the pain in her joints, she resolutely pushed all thought of failure and its trailing self-pity aside. This was something that had to be done. With her left hand she groped behind her for the back of the chair, but it was beyond her reach while she still leaned over the table. Thinking quickly, she stooped and managed to catch hold of the edge of the seat, and by exerting every ounce of her strength she pulled it around until the high wooden back lay under her fingers.

Thank God. Thank God for that. She could pause now for a rest. The erosion of her strength and mobility had been so gradual she hadn't fully realized until this very minute just how handicapped she had become. She bit her lip in frustration. They'd been very good, all the doctors, but there was nothing much they could do except dole out painkillers, walking-frames, calipers and drugs. They had even wanted to give her a chair that would lift her to her feet at the twist of a handle, but she couldn't imagine herself making use of that. 'What if it goes funny?' she asked at the clinic. 'I mean, I could get myself catapulted clear up to the ceiling.' The sister had laughed and tried to explain the impossibility of such an occurrence, but nothing she said could convince the old lady, so the offer had been quietly dropped.

Puffing a little now, Alice hung poised between the chair and the mantelpiece, her memories fading as her immediate needs pressed in on her. She had to get that fire turned back on before she froze to death. Greatly daring, she released her grip on the chair and let herself fall forward until she was able to transfer her grip to the ornate wooden mantel. The controls of the gas fire had been set high enough for her to reach without the need to bend, and a quick twist of the knob lit the jets. Finding the strength and courage to move back to the chair was a much tougher proposition. If she misjudged her distance and knocked the chair over she could be left clinging to the mantel all night.

It took all her determination and most of her strength before Alice had accomplished the journey from the hearth to the dining-chair, and from there to her armchair. She settled thankfully between its familiar arms, prepared to make the best of an uncomfortable night. It was no use trying to reach her bed, she'd decided with great regret, knowing full well that her strength would ebb the longer she was forced to sit, but there was no sense in doing too much. Besides, it wouldn't do to let Paul know how well she could manage. There was a chance he might overlook the fire being turned back on, but he'd never mistake which room he'd left her sitting in.

Alice fidgeted uncomfortably; she badly needed to spend a penny. In her efforts to overcome the rest of her problems she had almost managed to forget the demands of her bladder, but now the matter was urgent. She wriggled into a better position and was rewarded with a temporary respite. What could she do? There was the old commode in the bedroom, but she couldn't get to it, and the lavvy was out of the question. Paul had known she wanted to go when he left; he must have intended she'd be in this fix. She bit her lip and screwed her toes tightly against the soles of her slippers.

'Try not to think about it,' her mam used to tell her when she'd been caught short as a child. 'Screw your toes up and hang on till we get home.' But she wasn't going home. She wasn't going anywhere, and her insides felt as if they were bursting.

In desperation she clutched at herself. If she could only last out another few minutes the urge would pass over, she knew. She pulled a bunch in the front of her clothing, gathering the slack garments until she felt the woolly fabric of her knickers bite into her crotch. There, that was a bit better, she could hold it now. She eased back in the chair and was caught unaware as the hot flood burst forth, spreading up her back as it soaked into her clothing, and splashing down her legs to run into her slippers. Shame overwhelmed her. She'd never done such a thing in her life. Burying her face in her hands, she wept, brokenhearted.

With this latest indignity Alice abandoned herself to a fit of self-pity. Gone now were all her dreams and plans of making a new life for herself out in Australia with her Georgie. It had been madness at her age to even imagine such a thing could be possible. She was just a useless old woman. No wonder Georgie had never asked her to go out to him, he would know what he was letting himself and his family in for; thankless years spent caring for an incontinent cripple.

The glow given off by the gas fire lent a cosy light to the small room that belied the bleak, empty pain in Alice's heart. Who could she look to now for help and shelter? She would do better to resign herself to being locked away in some home for the rest of her life like so much worthless old rubbish.

The warmth of the room dried the small pool of urine,

the vapour rising with the air built up around the old lady until she, from constant inhaling, became mercifully unaware of its odour. From time to time she tried to flex her limbs and ease their cramped position, but the surge of blood that flowed along the squeezed old veins brought more pain than relief.

The wind changed during the night; blowing strongly now from the north-east, it found its way round the corner wall of the kitchen and spent its fury against the worn bricks at the back of the house. The temperature fell abruptly, and Alice was made even more uncomfortable as her still-damp stockings turned cold against the flesh of her legs. The chill struck deeper, slowing her thready pulse until her lower limbs became locked in frozen immobility.

And still the long night dragged on.

Dawn trailed in almost unnoticed, the shift from deep black to thick grey barely lifting the angular shapes of the furniture out from the shadows. Alice stirred, then winced in acute discomfort. She had dozed off and on throughout the seemingly endless night and she had little hope of any release from her torment until the children might come. She deliberately closed her mind to the long hours which must pass before their arrival. A little at a time, she told herself. Take it a little at a time. She felt ill now. Too ill to mind the squelching wet she'd sat in for hours. Too ill to notice the swollen flesh of her legs hanging like sausages over her slippers. Pain throbbed in her joints, jumping with every beat of her heart, knifing up through the bones of her skull, and tearing at the back of her eyes. She was too miserably ill to make any attempt to reach her medications, most of which were in the bedroom within easy reach of her bed, and how she longed for the comfort of that bed now. But it was too late, she was long past the time when she might have hoped to reach it by her own efforts.

The day wore on, bringing a flurry of freezing snow to beat on the panes behind the high back of Alice's chair. She turned dull eyes towards the sound of it and shivered even as she drew pathetic comfort from the steady hiss of the gas fire. At least she was spared the fear of meeting a slow end from the cold, she thought, making her first brave attempt at cheer since the day began. She even managed a wry smile when she recalled how alarmed she'd been when they'd changed her old coin-swallowing meter for one that seemingly ran all by itself. She'd never quite been able to grasp how they knew when to push the gas through the pipe if she didn't first signal her need by inserting the money. 'Thank the good Lord they did, though,' she uttered aloud, the impossibility of her getting up to feed coins into the slot, housed somewhere under the kitchen sink, coming forcibly home to her.

It was well past midday before the scrape of a key in the lock and the sound of the back door swinging open roused her from another pain-filled doze.

Ginger was first into the room, closely followed by a leather-jacketed creature whose lower limbs were encased in skin-tight jeans.

'She's here, Ma. I've brought her.' Flushed with pride, Ginger presented his girl-friend. Alice narrowed her eyes against the pain of focusing and beheld this strange apparition. A mop of multi-coloured hair teased and tormented into an outstanding halo crowned a face almost smothered in make-up. Shrewd orbs of light flicked beneath coated layers of black, taking stock of the shabby room and the state of its occupant before returned her gaze.

Shifting a wad of gum to the side of her mouth the girl gave a loud sniff before drawling, 'So this is the old dolly what's going ter show me the high life, is it?' She wrinkled her nose in disgust before rounding on the boy hovering anxiously beside her. 'Ginger, you crud. This heap of bones is only fit for the knackers.'

'No, listen, Freda. She's going ter take us up town, in a taxi, pay fer a meal and that. A real splash-out, the whole works.'

'No way, lover-boy. She's half dead, can't you see? And she's pissed herself, the dirty old bag.'

The biting contempt in her voice stabbed Alice into speech. 'I — I'm sorry, Ginger. I — its shameful you have to see me like this, but I — I —'

'Aw, come on, Ginger. Let's get out of here.' Freda stalked towards the door, giving Alice no time to finish what she was about to say. Ginger gaped after her.

'Hey, wait. We can't, Freda. Y'know what Paul said.'

'Oh, bugger Paul, and what he said. Who's he ter tell us what ter do?' She yanked at the door handle. 'Come on, will yer? I'm not stoppin' in this grotty hole.'

'Aw, Freda.' For a moment Ginger looked poised to follow after her, then his footsteps slowed as a thought took hold of his stumbling brain. 'Aw, Freda,' he called again, 'wait a bit, can't yer? I've got ter see Paul an' he'll be here in a sec.'

The rainbow mop reappeared round the door. 'Look, I've told yer. I'm not stoppin'. It might be all right fer you, but I could have more fun in a bleedin' morgue.'

'Well, can't yer just wait till Paul gets here? He's goin' ter pay me terday fer that last lot of stuff.'

'Big deal. And what happens then?'

'Then we can go out ter the Roadhouse an' have a rave-up.'

'Oh yeah? Like last time? Two rotten gins was all I got.'

'Okay, so I'll buy us a bottle. Then you can have as much as yer like.' Ginger was pleading now.

Faint interest showed on the painted face. 'Hmm. Maybe. I'm makin' no promises, but I'll be at the disco around eight. Tarrah fer now.' She wriggled her fingers in a mocking salute before slipping out of the house.

Ginger stared at the closed door, his usual good humour momentarily dashed. Scuffing his toes along the carpet, he ambled back to Alice. He longed with all his being to go after his girl, but his long-standing fear of Paul's temper and his dire need of funds held him fast.

'Yer frame's outside on the yard, did yer know?' he asked, without any real interest.

'I . . . I think Paul . . . I . . . Oh, dear.' The pain she was in was almost unbearable.

'What's up, Ma?' Her low groan drew Ginger's attention.

'Could you . . . Could you get me my pills, do you think?'

'Where are they? In yer bedroom? Ginger took his cue from her gesturing hand and went in that direction. He was gone only a second and returned to tip a collection of pill bottles in Alice's lap. 'There y'are, Ma,' he said with an air of bestowing treasure. 'I don't know which yer wanted so I brought 'em all.'

Alice groped among the bottles and located the one she needed with shaking hands. 'I'd like a drop of water, lad, if it's no trouble,' she begged as she shook out a double dose of her painkillers.

Ginger obligingly fetched a cup of water from the kitchen tap and, after handing it to Alice, trod restlessly round the small room. He was anxious to be off after Freda, but he knew it was no use going empty-handed. It had taken all his powers of persuasion to get her to come here with him today, and only his excited promise of a trip up to town had swayed her in his favour. He expected to get a tongue-lashing for the way things had turned out in any event, but if he had something to offer. . . His thoughts switched to the promise Paul had made him last night.

'Just get round ter Ma's termorrer,' he'd said, 'an' wait for me. I'll be seein' Steve ternight so I should have some bread for yer.'

Ginger's stomach had cramped violently. What if Ma had told him about their secret arrangement? He glanced quickly towards her now, his alarm returning.

'Yer won't let on ter Paul, will yer Ma? About us goin' up the town, I mean.'

'No, lad. No. I won't tell him, never fear.'

'Then promise. Promise yer won't.'

'I promise,' said Alice with as much assurance as she could manage. 'I'll never let on, so don't you worry.'

Ginger studied her carefully and was reassured. Nah, he was safe enough with Ma, he should have known. Hadn't even noticed he'd been a day late, he comforted himself. Clever that, the way he'd caught on to it bein' Sunday yesterday and all the shops shut. Course, it was Freda really who'd worked it all out. Some girl, his Freda. He resumed his restless pacing. Where the hell was Paul, he fretted. He'd promised he wouldn't be late.

'He hasn't already been, has he, Ma?' he asked in sudden alarm.

'Eh, what?' said Alice, startled out of a new doze.

'Paul. He hasn't been around yet terday?'

'No. No, not yet.'

'Not while you were in bed, like?'

'I haven't been to bed, son. I've been sitting here like this for I don't know how long.'

'Nah, come on, Ma. Yer can't 'ave been. You've been dreamin', I bet.' Ginger grinned at her, totally lacking the intelligence to comprehend her distressed condition.

'Aye, perhaps so,' sighed Alice, giving up the struggle to continue the argument. The strong drugs she had taken were knocking her out, but something nagged at the back of her mind. There was something she needed. Something she had to do. Oh, what was it? She turned her head restlessly, rolling it against the high chair-back. It was no use. She was too tired. Her eyelids drooped.

Ginger hated the silence. He threw himself into the

chair on the hearth and chewed savagely at his fingernails. Why didn't Paul come?

Alice's breathing grew deeper.

'Here, Ma.' Ginger shook the frail shoulder—'Here, if
yer goin' ter sleep yer'd better get off ter bed.'

Alice stared blearily into his freckled face. Bed? Yes,
that's what it was. She had to get to bed. Her hand
groped at the side of her chair. 'Frame, lad. I need my frame.'

'I told yer once, it's outside. Aw, hang on, I'll get it.' He
returned to place its frosted rails within the grasp of her
fingers.

The shock of the iced metal biting into her palms
brought Alice back to full consciousness with a gasp. 'By
God, lad. That's cold.'

'Yeah, it's freezin' out there,' said Ginger nonchalantly.

Alice fought to rise to her feet. This was a chance she
had scarcely dared hope for; bed meant rest, and rest
meant strength. She had to snatch at the opportunity.
Straining every ounce of her might, she struggled vainly
to rise from the chair. She couldn't straighten her legs.
Couldn't even feel her feet, and her arms would no longer
support her.

'It's no good. I can't.' Letting herself fall back, she was
obliged to admit defeat.

'C'mon. I'll give you a shove.' Ignoring her shrill cry of
alarm, Ginger stepped to the back of her chair and
pushed her into a near-standing position. Alice hooked
her fingers hysterically round the rails of the frame.

'No, I'll fall, I'll fall,' she screeched as the powerful arm
came round her waist, urging her to take a step. Terror
drove her leg forward and the first inch of her journey was
already accomplished.

Proud of his own ingenuity, Ginger pulled, pushed and
half-dragged her, sobbing with fright, into the bedroom.

'There,' he said as the bedside was reached. 'Now you'll
be okay.'

Alice could only continue to sob, racked with pain and a growing relief, as she was dropped to the bed.

'Aw, don't, Ma. There's nowt ter cry about.' Ginger hung over her for some minutes before turning away, drawn back to the warmth of the fire in the sitting-room.

Alice slowly recovered and managed to lift her legs up on to the bed, but she was unable to reach down to removed her slippers, which were now so tight on her swollen feet that they were causing her pain.

'In a bit,' she breathed, leaning back against the glorious softness of her pillows, 'I'll get them off in a bit.'

On his return to the sitting-room Ginger gathered up the bottles of pills that had spilled from Alice's lap and placed them on the table. His brow creased in concentration, he first attempted to read the labels, then he unscrewed the lids to sniff and poke at the contents. Re-capping the bottles, he sought to amuse himself by making a train of them and, chugging them back and forth across the tablecloth, he made several imaginary journeys.

Tiring at last of that occupation, he pushed the bottles into a heap and fell to gazing aimlessly round the shabby room until his attention was caught by the peculiar light from the narrow window. It was snowing heavily. Big, fat flakes that promised a heavy covering later. He crossed to the curtain and pulled it aside to get a better look. It'd be great tomorrow if this kept up, he thought with excitement. There'd be sledging on the big hill, maybe Barker's pond would freeze, he'd be able to try his hand at skating, perhaps.

A click from the wooden-framed clock as its finger passed the half-hour jerked him from his contemplation of the weather. Half past three. Where the bloody hell had Paul got to? Ginger kicked at the table leg in impatient frustration. He ought ter be here; he'd promised faithfully. Ginger gnawed at his finger-ends, indecision over what he should do if Paul didn't show up making him chew the already tender flesh to further destruction. He began pacing the hearth, pausing in his shambling stride only now and again to aim a vicious kick towards the legs of the pieces of furniture cluttering his promenade.

At four o'clock he decided he would hang about no longer. He'd go round to the coffee bar and find out if any of the crowd who hung about there had seen Paul. Taking care to re-lock the back door, he returned the key to its hiding place on the top of the lavatory cistern and set off, skating and sliding in the deepening snow.

CHAPTER 12

The brooding skies, so reluctant in giving birth to this day, had been pricked to depart by the spurs of the north-east wind, and had turned from the low slate roof under whose dubious protection Alice was waiting out the long night to cast about for more promising sport. It was rewarded where the tower blocks, edging the town with their concrete fingers, rose halfway to meet it. Here, in a council-subsidized eyrie, twenty-four flights above ground, a liquor-soused man roused from his sleep. His enormous hand, the fingers backed with bristling, black hairs, blundered across the seat of a chair, drawn up to serve as a table, at the side of the bed. Patting, groping, they searched across the sagging plastic and failed to discover their object. With a muttered curse the man threw back the bedclothes and swung his feet to the floor. Rubbing the slackness of sleep from his heavy jowls with a harsh rasp against the growth of his overnight beard, he hung over the edge of the bed while he gathered his senses. In the bed behind him a woman mewed in protest as the cold air crept in on her.

'Aw, Mick. Wasamarrer? Whatcha doin'?' she grumbled, opening one bleary eye as she hiked the covers up to her chin.

'Lookin' fer me fags.' The bedsprings twanged as he sifted his weight and stood erect. A craggy giant of a man, he topped six feet with inches to spare, his girth made even more formidable by the forest of black hair that covered every inch of his skin like a pelt. Naked, he lumbered towards the end of the bed and reached for his trousers, lying in an untidy heap where they had slid to the floor. With mounting irritation he rifled through the pockets until he located a cigarette packet. Flicking open the top, his irritation boiled into anger at finding it empty.

'Bloody stinkin' hell.' He hurled the packet across the room and began a destructive search amongst the pots, bottles and jars littering the powder-strewn surface of the dressing table.

The crash and clatter of glass meeting glass dragged the woman back from sleep.

'Hey! Whatcha think yer doin'? There's no rotten fags on there, is they? Use yer bloody loaf. Go an' get some off Paul,' she screamed at him, before flinging herself back on the bed and pulling the pillows over her head.

Mick snatched open the bedroom door, ducked his head to pass under the door frame, and cleared the narrow hallway beyond in a stride. He barged into the room which served as sitting-cum-dining room by day and Paul's bedroom when his mother and her paramour switched off the telly and retired for the night. Spotting the boy's clothing flung over a chair, Mick pounced on it and began to turn out the pockets. Sounds of his activity roused Paul, lying asleep on the narrow settee. He yawned and pushed himself up on one elbow to peer questioningly towards the disturbance.

'What the . . . ?' The man fixed a black stare at the boy as he slowly withdrew his hand from a pocket. Fast between his first two fingers emerged a wad of banknotes. 'Christ!' He dropped his gaze to stare at the money. 'Where the hell did yer get this?'

Fully awake now, Paul tried desperately to concoct a plausible story while swallowing the bile of his own stupid mistake. He was usually so careful to hide anything that might give away any hint of his illicit activities. Last night had been an exception. Last night he had been so late getting home he had almost blundered into his Mam and her bloke as they reeled along, arms intertwined, each propping the other up on their way back from the boozer. He had shot into the lift just a heartbeat ahead of them and had begun stripping off his clothing even as it ascended. Once through the door of the flat he'd lost no time in climbing under the old overcoat that did duty as his bedcover and had lain, feigning sleep when Mick and his Ma blundered through on their way to bed. He had been so relieved to escape castigation he had turned on his side and slept without giving further thought to the cash lining his pockets.

'Come on, stupid. I'm waitin'.' The man towered over him, the fist clenched over the notes brushing Paul's cheek. 'And don't give me no bloody lies or I'll beat yer 'ed in.'

'It's mine. I've bin savin' it,' was the best he could think of, faced with Mick's anger. A punch to the side of his head lifted him clear off the settee.

'I said no bloody lies, you deceitful little bleeder.'

Paul climbed to his feet and backed to the wall, a skeletal figure in grey underpants which had long forgotten ever being white.

'You've bin thieving again, 'aven't yer? 'Aven't yer?' Another blow to his head sent him sliding along the wall.

'What is it, Mick? What's all the row about?' His

mother, last night's make-up smeared in black and red blotches round her mouth and eyes, hung in the doorway.

'It's this bloody kid of yourn, look what I found in his pocket.' Mick waved the wad of notes under her nose. 'Sez he saved it, the lying little sod.'

'Aw, Paul. Where d'yer get it from? I hope you ain't bin doing nothing yer shouldn't. You know we can't afford to have no rozzers pokin' about here.'

Paul pressed himself further into the wall, his eyes never leaving Mick's face. He made no attempt to answer his mother.

'Leave him ter me, Jen. I'll get it out of him if I have ter kill him, so help me I will.'

Watching for his chance, Paul made a swift rush for the door, but the blowsy shape of his mother curtailed his escape.

Grabbing the boy by the hair, the man snapped him to and fro as if he was shaking a rug. 'Now tell me again where yer got all this money.'

'Piss off, why don't yer?' Paul managed to gasp out before a punch in his ribs knocked him to the floor. Crying tears of rage and frustration, he pushed himself up to a kneeling position. The man and woman stood silently watching. Suddenly the woman threw herself to her knees at his side.

'Come on, Paulie. Tell us where yer got it. Yer didn't pinch it, did yer? Not after last time.'

'Last time' was vivid in all their minds. Last time he'd been caught filching cash from clothing left by bathers in the lockers provided at the public swimming baths. The young constable called to the office where Paul was being detained by the baths officer had been moved to unprofessional pity by the sharply jutting bones and terrified mien of the undersized boy. His pity was further compounded when he lifted his hand to take Paul by the shoulder, for the boy shrank away in a manner that suggested he was expecting to receive a blow. The constable's eyes met those of the pool attendant and there passed between the two men a nod of understanding needing no words.

Paul intercepted the look and was inwardly cheered. It told him he had gauged his audience correctly, and it needed now only that suspicion of tears being bravely held back for him to win them over completely. It was only afterwards, when the Social Services came around asking questions, prodding and poking into his background, that he began to wish he'd taken a harder line with the copper. Better a fine and a caution from some batty old judge than all this interference with his private life. Nor was that all. When it was discovered his Mam had a 'friend' who lived in, the Housing Department were prompt on the scene with a threat of eviction unless her 'friend' was swift to move out. Their agreement of tenancy included no lodgers. What use for his Mam to protest that Mick was her fiancé, when that had brought hasty investigation from the Social Security, coupled with suspension of her weekly benefit.

With each fresh official came a beating from Mick, who bitterly resented this havoc wrought on the cushy little number he'd secured for himself. It had taken several months for all the fuss to die down, last time, and all three of them remembered it. Mick had actually been obliged to move out, then Paul's Mam had taken over the beatings, venting her fear of losing her man, and the frustration of enforced celibacy, in the vigour of wielding the strap. When Mick had eventually judged it safe to return Paul had been doubly careful to keep a low profile—and now this!

'Shift out, Jen. I'll make him tell us.' Mick stooped and jerked Paul aloft by his ankles, dangling him upside down like a rabbit about to be skinned. Across the room to the glass door letting on to the balcony he went, with Paul no weight in his muscular grip. Without breaking his stride he stepped on to the balcony, suspended two hundred feet above ground, and swung the boy out over the side.

Blind, gut-searing terror screamed through Paul's frame, locking his mind and his body alike in a rigid convulsion.

'No, Mick. No. Pull him back. Oh, Christ, you'll kill him.' His mother leaned out to see him hanging, stiff as a board, held by one leg.

'I'll kill him all right if he gives me any more lip. I wouldn't mind bettin' it were him as made off with that steak I brought fer yesterday's dinner. He deserves killin'.' With a final angry shake of the limb he was holding, Mick straightened to full height, lifting Paul back into the room and letting him fall with a thud to the floor. Semiconscious with shock, only a whimper escaped him.

'Now tell me yer saved it, if yer dare.' Seeing the boy was unable to answer, Mick resumed his search for cigarettes, and, finding a packet in Paul's jacket pocket, extracted one and lit it before prodding the quaking form with his toe. 'Well. Where's it from, then?'

Paul shook violently in the grip of a nervous reaction, his teeth clacking together in spite of the vomit oozing out of his mouth. 'P . . . p . . . pin . . . I . . .'

'Aw, fer cryin' out loud, Jen. Get him a whisky or summat, I'll be here all bloody day at this rate.' Mick dropped into a chair and drew deeply on the cigarette, his total nakedness passing unremarked by the woman who shuffled off to do his bidding. 'And see what's fer breckers while you're about it,' he called after her as she disappeared into the kitchen.

She came back holding a cup, which she took a swallow from before extending it towards Paul, who continued to writhe on the floor, the shaking having now given way to racking sobs.

'Here, Paulie. Drink this.' She pushed the cup under

his nose. Paul took it in both hands and struggled to drink. He needed no further persuasion from Mick. The neat whisky Paul choked down in heaving gulps set him babbling the moment it hit his empty stomach.

He told them how he'd set up his network, starting off on his own, then getting the others to steal to his requirements. He described in detail how he sold the stuff they had stolen to a guy he'd met who ran a stall at a Sunday flea-market. On and on he babbled, giving Mick the names of all his recruits. He told him of Alice, making her fondness for himself and his companions sound like interfering patronage.

'Old Ma, we call her.' He choked on the name. 'Mrs bleedin' Maxwell.' He flinched away as Mick raised his fist at his use of the expletive. 'A right old ma, she is, an' all. But we've had her fooled good and proper between us.'

A whining bravado crept into the lengthy recital as he detailed the way he and the others had made free use of Alice's home. Mick's eyes narrowed as the boy went on with his story and he sucked a sharp breath through clenched teeth. Christ! This was a whole lot worse than he'd ever anticipated when he began his questioning.

He had been prepared for no more than admission of theft, something he could have whaled the daylights out of the young bugger for, but this! This was something else. He was out of his depth, he couldn't afford the police nosing round, and there was no way of knowing that the other kids wouldn't lead them this way. Not much use going to see their parents to get them to warn their brats to keep their traps shut, either. They might think he was trying to pass off Paul's share of the blame. Might even be one of them stupid enough to go to the cops themselves, you never knew with folks these days.

Rage and frustration coursed through him. 'You stupid little bastard.' He spat the words at Paul, his lips drawn back in a snarl. 'Ain't we got enough damn aggro without you makin' more?' Unable to contain himself any longer, his fists shot out, smashing towards the boy's face and chest.

Paul went down under the onslaught, his arms raised in a feeble attempt to protect his head. Blood spurted from his nose and lips and a searing pain stabbed through his ribs.

'Stop it, Mick, for God's sake—' Paul's mother grabbed for the raised fist—'and go and get some clothes on.'

The upraised arm made contact with a pillow of soft flesh as she drew it down, the warmth of her generous breasts pressing against the flimsy nylon gown she wore searing his already inflamed senses. Turning, he caught her savagely in his arms, straining her body against him.

Paul became dimly aware of their writhing, panting forms flailing on the carpet beside him. He drew his knees up to his chest, shrinking from contact with their heaving bodies. He hated her. He hated him. He hated them both, the dirty, stinking bastards.

Their senses replete, the pair made no immediate effort to remove themselves from the boy's vicinity but lay panting heavily, bodies still intertwined in a sweaty embrace. Without getting up from the floor Mick stretched an arm in the direction of Paul's discarded jacket, dragged it towards him, and fumbled his second packet of cigarettes from one of its pockets, the beefy fingers all but bursting the narrow opening.

'Bloody hell.' He let the pack fall and dipped again and again into the pocket. 'Will yer look at all these?' he asked the woman, who, disturbed by his movements, had pushed herself into a sitting position.

'What's up now?' she asked over her shoulder.

'These, look. All these sodding fags.' Mick continued to produce cigarettes from the folds of Paul's jacket. 'I bet he's swiped these an' all. Little bleeder.' The pile mounted alongside the man's naked thigh until he had emptied the jacket pockets of all but the dirty, torn linings. He gave the coat a final dust-raising shake before flinging it from him. 'You're gonna have ter do summat about that bloody kid, I'm tellin' yer, Jen,' he said as he tore the wrapping from one of the packets and extracted a cigarette.

'Like what?' she asked in a flat, bored tone. The face she turned towards him over her bare shoulder had not been improved by their recent activities; the blue eye-shadow lay in greasy furrows that stretched out from the bridge of her nose almost to the tip of her ears, and black mascara had crept downwards through the sweat beading her face to lie like broken spider's legs on her cheeks.

The slack flesh of her jaw and chin was mercifully hidden by her upraised shoulder, but even Mick's hardened stomach had witnessed enough.

'Festering hell, Jen. Can't yer do summat about your bloody face?' He withdrew his legs from their contact with hers. 'Go and get a wash, can't yer?'

Jen jerked her head angrily, bringing the bleached hair down over her eyes.

'That suit yer?' she demanded. 'Bloody particular all at once, aren't we?'

'Oh, sod off.' Mick planted his foot in the small of her back and gave it a shove.

'Don't you tell me ter sod off, you bloody pig. You're no rotten oil paintin' yersen.' She swiped wildly at the offending foot.

'Huh. It's not oil paint as you need, not wi' all that jallop on yer mug.'

The woman turned suddenly and came at him on her hands and knees, her full breasts swinging between her arms and impeding her progress.

Dropping his unlit cigarette, Mick grabbed at her with both hands and heaved her on top of him. Burying his hands deep in her hair, he dragged her face down to his chest and rubbed it vigourously into the coarse matted hair.

'Now get on with what you're best at,' he ordered, freeing one hand to squeeze and knead at the ripe, heavy breasts.

Paul squinted across the narrow gap now separating him from their copulating forms, tears of rage and disgust running down his face to mingle with the blood and mucus oozing from his nose and mouth.

As the sound of their breathing mounted, grew rasping and ragged, he slapped at his ears, rocking himself to and fro in a desperate attempt to shut out the nauseous, pulsating sound that seemed to beat back at him from every wall of the room.

CHAPTER 13

A gnawing hunger tugged at Alice's senses, pulling her from the comforting arms of sleep. Where was she? Her groping fingers explored the quilt and identified its worn surface. Oh, yes. Now she had it, she was in her own bed. But why? What was she doing here? As she attempted to change her position the throbbing ache in her joints jumped into protesting pain. Fragments of memory returned, and for a weak moment she was tempted to stay where she was. To lie still in the soft bed, cushioning her hurts. She was defeated. Too worn to fight any more.

I'm too old for all this, she defended herself. Relaxing into the cocoon of warmth, she allowed herself the luxury of drifting towards a light doze, until her griping stomach demanded some action and she struggled into a sitting position. Lord but she was hungry. Rubbing her middle, she looked towards the luminous face of the alarm clock.

Five to ten. But five to ten, when? Morning? Night? And what day? Panic threatened to swamp her as she realized that she had no idea.

'Now, this won't do,' she muttered resolutely. Feeling carefully along the top of the bedside table, she located the lamp and switched it on. 'Must be night,' she said, noting the strength of the shadows. Now, which night? No matter how she cudgelled her brains there was no way she could tell. Was it Monday, maybe? Or Tuesday? Or was it later on in the week than that? At last her machinations produced some result and she sagged back against the headboard as a depressing piece of the puzzle was slotted into place. All her attempts to gain Ginger's help had come to nothing and she was back where she had started. Well, then, I'll just have to think of something else, she told herself firmly, ignoring the hopeless voice that asked mockingly . . . Like what?

At the moment her hunger was her most pressing problem and she decided that she would feel better, be more able to make some fresh plans, once she'd got some food inside her. Her walking-frame stood by the bed and she reached towards it. By the time she had managed to climb down from the bed to try her weight on her still-swollen feet, she knew she would never accomplish her intended journey through to the pantry. Letting herself sink back on to the bed, she pondered her fate. Oh, if only she wasn't so hungry, and she was getting thirsty now, too.

Sitting on the edge of the bed, her fingers gripping the rail of her walking-frame, she lowered her head on to her arms. Was this to be the end of her, then? Left here to starve in her own home by a group of thoughtless children? 'No, by golly, I won't.' Alice straightened her spine as she made her brave declaration. If she wasn't totally out in her reckonings there should be a bottle of milk sitting outside on the windowsill of this very room, that would keep her going all right, milk was a marvellous source of energy. Eyeing the distance from where she was sitting to the window, Alice saw what she must do in order to reach her objective. First she would lift the walking-frame on to the bed. Then she would have to roll both the frame and herself over to the far side. From there it was less than a yard to the window.

She had thought no further than getting the milk bottle into her hands by the time the pain-filled scramble across the billowing quilt was accomplished. It wasn't until she set her feet on the floor below the sill that a further possibility suggested itself. She could use the milk bottle as a means of getting away from here. It could be her lifeline. All she need do was pop a note into it once it was empty, and the milkman would do all the rest.

Almost sick with excitement at the prospect of getting immediate help, Alice was tempted to pour away its precious contents, the quicker to gain the empty bottle. But she fought down the temptation, gathered her wits about her, and forced herself to sit on the edge of the bed with the full bottle in hand. There are hours to go yet before the milkman is due with the next delivery, and you will need all your strength; now, drink, she ordered.

Lifting the chill glass neck to her lips, she began taking steady sips. As the level of milk fell, Alice planned her next move. She would need paper and pencil, of course. That was the first thing. But where was she to get it? The pad she had used when she'd accidentally started this whole nightmare off by trying to send a note to the police station was in the sitting-room along with her pen, and she had no hope of getting through to fetch them. So where was she to find another?

Setting the half-empty bottle back on the sill, she struggled along the length of her bed to the dressing-table filling the room's corner. The remains of an indelible pencil she'd last used years ago for marking her laundry came to light as she fished through its many drawers, and she seized on it with a positive chortle of glee. 'Now, you are just what I need,' she told it, wetting its point with the tip of her tongue while searching deeper into the back of the drawer for something she could write on.

Old birthday cards and valentines tied into bundles with scraps of satin ribbon were lifted lovingly to one side. She could never bring herself to deface one of those, no matter how urgent her need. They went back all the way through the years to the days when she and her Sid were first walking out. Just to have them under her fingers brought the memories flooding back. Ah, they didn't make cards like these any more, not if the garish, and often downright rude, pieces of nonsense she had seen in the shops were anything to go by, they didn't. Why, some of these beautiful cards were works of art in themselves.

Sliding a yellowed oblong of ivory from the top of a bundle, she examined again the hand-painted violets it displayed. They still looked so real for all their sixty-odd years; she could almost smell their soft fragrance.

To the top of the pile now was a birthday greeting of red roses punched in relief on a tablet of tissue-fine celluloid. The old fingers caressed the twists and turns of the design, feeling their way over the skilfully wrought petals before opening the paper backing to read; 'For my beloved Alice, on her first birthday as my adored wife.' None of the beautiful sentiment expressed in the printed verse that followed moved her as much as those simple hand-written words. Oh, if only her Sid could be here with her now.

Placing the cards gently back in their place, Alice continued her search, certain there must be a scrap of paper somewhere that she could write on. At last she was obliged to tear a piece off the paper lining the drawer; it was rather flimsy and a little bit crumpled, but it would just have to do. Now then, what should she put? 'Please send help, I'm being held prisoner.' Would that be enough? Ought she to say her life was in danger, or was that going too far? A cautious but none the less urgent, 'I am very ill, please send help quickly,' finally won favour, and she pencilled the message with trembling hands.

Deciding against putting her note under the empty bottle for fear it would get overlooked, Alice rolled it loosely and slipped it into the neck. There, surely it would be seen poking out of the bottle like that. She made yet another laborious journey to the window and stood the empty in the usual place on the sill. Before she lowered the pane on its sashcord she glanced out into the night. The snow had stopped falling and it was now freezing hard. Alice shivered as she climbed back into bed and pulled the quilt round herself. It was her intention to stay awake for what remained of the night and wait for the milk-float to pull up at her door. She was determined to be ready to leave when the milkman should knock in response to her note. An hour passed, then another, before she indulged in the luxury of closing her eyes; just for a second or two, she promised herself; only to be swept immediately into a deep sleep.

A wind from the west tempered the frost and brought a shower of rain to pit the smooth blanket of snow. It fluttered the flimsy paper sticking out of the bottle until an extra large raindrop hammered it deeper into the neck, putting an end to the wind's game. The wind tumbled away in the early hours, trailing another keen frost in its wake, to peak the splashes of rain and set all the world in its icing. The milkman, huddled deep into his assortment of woollen pullovers, trundled his float over this perilous surface. He spotted the bottle, now white with frost, and cursed as he skidded past. He'd only been put on this round temporarily, the regular man had gone down with the flu, and he resented the extra yards that calling on Alice added to his journey.

'Not as if they ever want more than a couple of bottles a

week,' he grumbled aloud as he gingerly trod from his float to her door. 'Some of these old 'uns have more cheek than a pig's face, the way they expect waitin' on.' Snatching the empty away from the bond the weather had formed with the sill, he exchanged it none too gently for a full one, then slithered back to his float. The crash of the empty bottle striking the base of the crate gave him a moment of grim satisfaction before he released the handbrake and crept on his way.

Alice stirred and muttered drowsily, cocooned in the warmth of the quilt. 'Got to be ready,' she mouthed, ignorant of the passage of time since she'd closed her eyes. 'Must be ready,' her tone was firmer now as sleep receded. Yawning, she blinked her eyes to clear their weak watering and turned her gaze towards the window. A narrow oblong, only slightly less dark than the surrounding wall, wavered in her vision. Won't be long now, she thought. It's getting light at last. Pushing away the quilt's drugging warmth, she sat up and switched on the lamp. It was just coming up to six thirty. Had she better be getting into her coat? She eyed the big wardrobe dubiously. It looked a long, long way from the bed, and her limbs were stiff and unresponsive. No, she'd leave it. The milkman would maybe get it for her.

Patiently she waited. Couldn't be long now. Tilting her head to one side, she listened, hoping to catch the chink of bottles that would herald the milk-float's arrival. Her eyes turned continually to the clock. Six forty-five, seven o'clock, seven fifteen. At seven thirty she pushed herself to the edge of the bed and lowered her feet to the floor. From here she could no longer see the blank-faced alarm with its uncaring hands. What difference did it make what time it was? Milk could be late arriving, just the same as anything else, couldn't it?

By eight o'clock she was unable to pretend any longer. The milk just wasn't coming. Sick disappointment made it impossible for her to sit still. Pulling her walking-frame closer, she levered herself upright and half fell, half stepped forwards to prop herself against the windowsill. Pulling aside the curtain, she peered through the tracings left by the frost. The same frost had worked on the waiting milk bottle with mischievous fingers, turning the white fluid into lumpy crystals, pulling them up into a mound out of the bottle neck. Alice pushed up the window and stared in disbelief at her silent accuser.

With part of her mind she registered its condition and knew that it must have been standing there for some hours. Hours. While you, you foolish old woman, have slept away your last chance, she berated herself. Her physical condition was worsening, and she knew that once she got back to the bed she would not have the strength to move from it unaided again. Alice couldn't prevent the sob that escaped her. How could she have been so stupid? Tears blinded her eyes. She lifted the bottle inside, a vague prayer — that she'd been mistaken, that this was the bottle containing her note, and the milkman was yet to come — dissolving as she felt the weight of it. The iced surface slipped through her fingers and she watched the bottle fall, striking her walking-frame and shattering. Frozen milk fell with a splodge amongst the cruelly curved shards of glass, but Alice no longer saw, and she no longer cared. Despair washed over her. Clinging to the window's edge she gave way to bitter tears.

The thud of heavy feet echoing from the covered entry failed to register on Alice's ears, as did the shudder of protest from the back door under the stress of a hefty kick that sent it crashing open. It wasn't until Ginger catapulted into her bedroom that Alice became aware of anything outside of her own helpless misery.

'She's chucked me. My Freda. She's chucked me and it's all your bloody fault.' The round freckled face, now puce with temper, was thrust forwards from the bull neck.

Alice stared in mystification.

'You promised us a day on the town, a treat, you said. An' look what we got.' The cracked voice was almost a scream, and the taunts of his girl-friend rang anew in his ears.

He'd chased all over town last night trying to find Paul. When it got to nine o'clock he'd plucked up his courage and gone round to the flat, something Paul had made him swear he'd never do, but he had been desperate. He had to lay hands on some money; Freda would be waiting for him down at the disco. There had been no answer to his repeated knocking until his knocks had turned to furious two-fisted blows that jarred the door in its frame. Then other doors along the landing had been pulled open by the neighbouring tenants demanding to know what all the noise was about. Ginger had taken one hasty look round the ring of irate faces before he turned and fled down the stairwell, in too great a hurry to wait for the lift.

By the time he reached the disco his wild race across town was very much evident in the heaving chest, the gaping shirt collar, and the sweat trickling down from his damp hair.

Willie Barnes, the man who kept the door at the old cinema turned bingo-hall turned disco, had refused him admission.

'But I've got ter get in. Me girl's waitin' for me in there,' Ginger panted.

'Not without payin' yer don't,' Willie told him.

'Just ter see her, I won't stop,' Ginger pleaded.

'Sorry. No admission without a ticket. And no ticket without yer pays fer it.' Willie remained notably unmoved by the tortures of adolescent love.

Ginger took a threatening step towards him, which halted mid-stride as Willie rose in a businesslike manner and pushed back his chair.

'Well, can't yer just tell her I'm here?' Ginger pleaded.

'Can't leave the door, can I?'

'Aw, shit.' Ginger kicked his toe viciously against the tiled steps. He didn't know what to do now. Freda would be furious with him if he stood her up and even more furious when she found out he'd got no money. Thrusting his hands deep in his pockets, Ginger turned back into the street. 'I'll get yer fer this one of these days,' he promised Willie over his shoulder.

'Hey, Ginge! Are you looking for Freda?' a voice called from the disco. Ginger whipped round to see two girls on the point of descending the steps.

'Yeah,' he answered eagerly. 'Is she in there?'

'No, she left ages ago. She was ever so mad.' The girls exchanged knowing grins and one of them started to giggle.

'Where's she gone?' asked Ginger, a disappointed ache hitting his belly.

'Tell him, Sue. Tell him.' The giggling girl elbowed her friend in the ribs.

'Aw, shut up, Claire.' Suddenly uncomfortable under the scrutiny of the overgrown boy, the girl shrugged and pretended elaborate loss of interest. Spotting a group of youths further down the street, she sought her escape. 'Hey, look. There's Chalkie's gang.' She tugged urgently at her friend's arm. 'Let's go and see where they're off to.' With a toss of her head for Ginger, she flounced by, leaving him to stare helplessly with a sigh after their departing figures. He turned himself about and trailed aimlessly up the street, not knowing where to go now to find Freda. He plodded the streets until his feet were wet and numb with cold, then he made for his home, having decided to go round to Freda's home early the next day and catch her as she left for school. He'd swear to make it up to her for tonight. He was bound to see Paul tomorrow, he reasoned, and with the money he was to receive he'd really be able to get back into Freda's good books.

He was awake early and up and dressed without his mother having to yell and shout for him to 'get up before the sun scorches your eyes out' as she normally did. He wolfed his breakfast and tore out of the house without stopping to register the time. It was far too early for him to have a hope of meeting Freda, so he hung about the street outside her home until he saw first her dad, then her mum, leaving for work. It was bitterly cold, and he hopped from one foot to the other, jogging up and down in an effort to keep warm. He watched the house carefully and was presently rewarded by the sight of his Freda as she passed the window. Greatly daring, he unlatched the front garden gate and strode across the yard of snow-covered mud which, in the summer, went under the guise of a lawn. His heart beat a rapid tattoo of anticipation as he hammered on the door.

Freda gawped at him in a mixture of disgust and amazement. 'What the hell are you doin' here?' she demanded, making no effort to ask him inside.

'I wanted ter see yer. Ter tell yer—'

'Ter tell me what a great time we're goin' to have. Like we did at that dirty old bag's yesterday?' Freda cut in scathingly. 'Or like we had last night when you didn't even turn up?'

'Nooo. Aw, Freda, listen,' Ginger wailed.

'I'm not listening to you no more, Ginger Hargreaves. You're all wind and piss, you are.' Freda made to close the door in his face, but Ginger shot out a detaining hand.

'No, wait. Listen. I love yer, Freed.'

'Love me! What d'you know about love? Yer great gormless lump.' Her gaze raked him, from the uncombed hair, its carroty hue clashing disastrously with his frost-reddened nose, down past the huge nail-bitten hands to the scuffed toes of his shoes. Her upper lip curled. 'You make me sick, you do,' she said at last. 'Come with me to Ma's, you said. We'll have a ball, you said. An' then what happens? I get dragged to a doss-house an' stood up in the friggin' disco. That's what happens.'

'That wasn't my fault, Freed. Paul didn't turn up with me money.'

'Well, if it's Paul that's got all the bread, I'd be better off with him, then, wouldn't I?'

'But you can't, Freed. He's just a bloody kid an' I love yer, I really do love yer.'

'Look, piss off, Ginger. And don't come round me no more. I've had enough of yer rabbitin', playin' the big time and nowt at the back of it.' She snatched the door from his grasp. 'So just sod off, why don't yer?' she yelled. Then the door had slammed shut, leaving Ginger blinking back tears of hurt and bewilderment.

He loved her. He'd never love anybody else, he mourned as he stared at the closed door. For a moment he was tempted to knock on it again; to make another attempt at pleading his case; but the memory of that long, raking look stayed his hand. It was then his thoughts turned on Alice. He needed someone to blame for his hurt, and it was her fault his Freda had ditched him, wasn't it? Swinging about, he strode off in the direction of her home. His wounded pride and growing sense of loss churned up inside him as he slithered over the ice-covered pavements. By the time he reached Alice's door his choking self-pity had turned into the burning rage that sent him hurtling into her bedroom.

As Alice stared from her place at the window, he advanced across the room.

'Why couldn't yer have done like yer said, then everything would have bin all right?' Ginger skirted the bed to tower over her. Not a word left her lips. 'Well, say summat,' Ginger screeched.

Alice trembled in her effort to understand why all this

venom should be so directed at her. She opened her mouth but was helpless to force any words past her dry tongue. What could she say? What did he want? She remained clinging weakly to the windowsill while the force of his anger buffeted about her.

By now Ginger was lost to all reason. He had cherished Freda in his own simple fashion, adored her. Having a girl of his own had given him a status he'd never reached before. Now she was gone. He'd been given the brush-off.

The pain of his loss seared through him and his fingers closed into a fist that lifted almost without his volition. Thwarted desire brought his arm crashing down, to sweep Alice like a dead leaf from the sill to the floor.

'It's your fault. It's all your bloody fault.' Ginger wept openly now as the dam of his anger gave way. Tear-blinded, he blundered into the bed as he made his way from the room. Kicking his feet free of the hanging quilt, he shouldered his way through the door.

The tears continued to fall as he relocked the outer door and returned the key to its place. He scrubbed at his eyes with the sleeve of his anorak as he turned into the entry and charged through into the street, loud wet snuffles marking his passage.

CHAPTER 14

Collecting up the case records for her impending day's visits, Betty Kent discovered a slip of paper folded over the face of the lower one. 'Check on Mrs Maxwell, 79, Princess Street,' she read. It was printed in her own hand. Mrs Maxwell? Who was that? Oh, yes. She remembered her now and also remembered her own half-formed intention to call again on the old lady when she was next out on that side of town.

'Marion, what do you know about a Mrs Maxwell, living out on Princess Street?' She leaned back on her chair, tilting it up on two legs as she directed her question across the office to her colleague, who pursed her lips thoughtfully before she made her reply.

'Not a lot, I don't think. Wasn't she the old dear who wouldn't move out when the council wanted to rehouse? And didn't we get the job of trying to persuade her?'

'Yes, that's the one.' Betty picked up a paperclip and began to straighten its curves.

'Well, that's about all I know of her. She's not one of ours, is she?'

'Not strictly speaking. She's in our area but she's not on the books.' The paperclip was now in the process of becoming a letter B. 'I called round there the other day. I was out on my rounds and suddenly I thought I'd look in. Very independent old lady, I liked her . . . only . . . I couldn't help feeling . . . Betty tilted her head and studied her handiwork as she turned her letter B into a shepherd's crook. 'I felt a bit . . . um—'

'Oh, no. Don't! You and your feelings. I keep telling you, we are not paid to feel.'

'Ah, and you never do, of course,' said Betty, her obviously teasing tone belying her words as she snapped the clip in two and tossed the pieces away. 'You have a heart of stone, hate all the clients, heartily approve of corporal punishment, and wouldn't stick at bashing an old lady or two. 'Spect you think Mrs Maxwell ought to be left to get on with her own affairs.'

'S'right,' Marian muttered agreeably, her head buried in the pile of folders covering her desk.

'All the same, I think I'll just look in on her if I get time today,' Betty said thoughtfully, bringing her chair safely back to four legs and standing up. 'Can't do any harm.'

It was snowing again before she completed her official visits and turned her car into the crumbling remains of

Princess Street. Driving carefully along the steep camber, she slowed to a halt opposite the lone house and got out of her car. Everything looks normal enough, she thought, as she picked her way across the snow and ice to Alice's front door. Remembering her previous instructions, she didn't stop to knock, but stepped into the covered entry and made her way round the back. Getting no answer to her repeated knocking, she tried the door and was vaguely disturbed to find it was locked. Cupping her hands to her eyes, she peered through the window into the sitting-room. The gas fire was burning, lending enough light for her to see that the room was empty. With a shrug for her fears, Betty turned to leave. Funny, she had no reason to suspect there was anything wrong, but the same niggle of doubt that had brought her here in the first place made her pause as she emerged from the entry into the street.

Feeling a little foolish, she hoisted herself on to her toes in order to bring her face close to the glass in the high-set front window. The room was in darkness but she could pick out the dim shape of the bed and the wardrobe and she saw nothing to cause her to take any further action. Dropping back to her heels, she stood for a moment contemplating the front door.

Should she knock? There seemed little point when she knew the house to be empty. She chewed worriedly at her lower lip. Where on earth could the old lady have gone? She couldn't possibly be out in the loo, could she? But no, Betty was unable to persuade herself to accept so simple an explanation. People didn't lock the back door behind them when they went to the toilet, did they? Wait a minute, though. What day was today? Tuesday. Could she have gone to collect her pension? Betty frowned in concentration. No-o. She didn't think Tuesday was Mrs Maxwell's day for that. She stared again at the uncommunicative door. Why can't you talk, she thought at it crossly. Then I wouldn't need to stand here in this filthy stuff wondering what I should best be doing.

Oh, I think I'll go back to the office and just forget it, was her next irritable resolve, her dismay at Alice's absence prodding her previously vague worries into real niggles of doubt that created in her an unaccustomed impatience. She half turned to go, then thought better of it and headed back up the entry. She paid particular attention to the rear view of the house as she rounded the lavatory wall and stepped on to the snow-covered back yard. Everything looked absolutely normal. She stared intently at the upper windows and the empty shell of the adjoining houses. No, they looked even more innocent than usual under their white covering. Beating her hands together to drive out the creeping cold, Betty turned back to the lavatory door; with a half-apologetic glance over her shoulder she pushed it open and looked into the small space. Well, at least there was nothing alarming in there. Letting out her breath in a relieved sigh, she turned yet again into the entry and emerged to stare once more at the front door.

'Oh well, why not,' she muttered as she rapped on it sharply. An echoing silence mocked her persistence. The snow was coming heavily now and she grimaced up into the swirling flakes, taking off her headscarf and shaking it free of its damp burden before crossing the narrow road and getting back into her car. With a sigh of resignation she fitted the ignition key and turned it. A final glance across at the house, now almost completely obliterated by the falling snow, convinced her she'd better get back to the main roads while she still could. These old, steeply cambered side-streets offered no purchase for small modern cars. Her rear wheels spun, slipping the car sideways, before the nearside tyre struck the edge of the kerb and gave her enough of a jolt to start the car into forward motion. Allowing it to creep along at a cautious pace, Betty probed her anxiety at finding the house empty.

The old lady could have gone to stay with one of her children, she supposed. Perhaps she paid them frequent visits. Perhaps she was ill, or maybe the weather . . . Of course. That was the most likely explanation, the snow. The old lady wouldn't be able to get about in this stuff, not even with the aid of that walking-frame, and she had no doubt left the gas fire burning to keep the house aired, stop the pipes from freezing. Betty felt quite happy with this interpretation and, relieved of her most immediate worry, turned all her attention to steering a reasonably straight course.

Drifting on the gentle waves of a deepening coma, Alice lay where she had fallen, all unaware that help had briefly stretched out its hand, then passed on its way.

The snow cushioned the sound of the children's booted feet as Elaine and Tony turned into the street in hot pursuit of the fleeing John. A bright red patch on Tony's temple and the clods of snow caught in his clothing told their own tale of an accurately dispatched snowball.

'Get him, Tone. Go on, get him.' Elaine dropped out of the race, clutching at her side. 'Chuck a snowball at him,' she panted.

Trying to keep a backward watch over his shoulder, John lost his footing on the treacherous surface and fell sprawling across Tony's path. The younger boy ploughed into him, snow and fists flying. Elaine forgot the stitch in her side and lumbered along to add her weight to the mêlée, which had by now carried the combatants to Alice's front doorstep. Their whoops and shouts added renewed savour to the fight as they stuffed handfuls of frozen snow into each other's necks and faces.

'Aw, pack it in. Pack it! I'm bloody wet through.' John tried in vain to roll from under Elaine's superior weight.

'Watcher think we are?' she yelled back at him, reaching for another scoop of snow.

'Hey! Look out. Look out, Elaine. It's all going ter come down off the roof.' Tony scuttled crabwise along the gutter as he shouted his warning. The heavy snow overhung the roofing slates in a threatening sweep. Elaine and John broke off hostilities to stare upwards. 'Come on, shift! Get out of the way,' Tony shrilled needlessly as the pair slithered and scrambled to a safe vantage point.

'Wow. I bet that lot 'ud squash yer flat if it fell on yer,' Elaine observed with relish.

'Yeah,' breathed John appreciatively. They stood in silence, necks craned back, for some minutes.

'It's not goin' ter fall.' There was disappointment in John's tone.

'Betcha!' Tony declared.

'Tell yer what. Let's see if we can knock it down.' John began gathering snow into a ball, and the others, no less eager, were quick to follow suit.

Despite their best efforts they were unable to dislodge the massed weight of hanging snow.

'Aw, let's go in an' get dry, my feet are freezin',' Tony complained, losing interest in the project, and he stamped up and down while he waited for his companions to give up their fruitless exercise.

'Come on, then.' Elaine dispatched her last snowball roofwards and stepped into the covered entry.

The three of them charged across the back yard to collide with a chorus of grunts and gasps as the door held firm against them.

'Open the bloody door, then.' John shouldered Elaine aside and made a grab at the old-fashioned brass doorknob.

'It's locked,' Elaine informed him flatly as he twisted the knob backwards and forward.

'Why is it?'

'How the hell should I know?' she yelled.

Tony stood by looking from one to the other of them.

'Where's the key?' he asked.

John and Elaine turned first to stare at him, then at each other. Their faces wore expressions of blank surprise. They'd never known this door to be locked against them and had never questioned the possible need for a key.

John shrugged aside his surprise and was quick to assume a superior air. 'I expect Paul locked it. No sweat, he'll have left the key for us somewhere.'

'Like where?' Elaine asked crushingly.

'Like in the loo, or somewhere.' said John all ready to pick a fresh fight. He turned in the direction of the outside lavatory. A sound like a giant sigh, followed by a heavy drumming, held him in mid-stride.

'The snow.' Tony and his sister shouted in unison before dashing out of the yard towards the entry. John followed just in time to see the last of the roof-load fall on to the shoulder-high pile outside Alice's window.

'Hey, just look at it.' Tony stared in round-eyed amazement. The past few days had brought the heaviest snowfall he'd seen in all his eight years, and the glistening mound towering above his head held him fixed in wonder.

'Come on. Don't just stand gawpin'. Let's make us an igloo,' cried John, launching himself at the white mass.

Their shrill excited cries penetrated the fog shrouding Alice's senses. She heard them without waking. The children were near, she could hear them. She waited for them to come in. They'd maybe have a bit of her fresh currant cake for their tea. A little half-smile touched her lips, and peace smoothed the care from her brow. She turned happily back to the comforting waves.

'What time d'yer reckon it is?' Elaine peered towards John, suddenly aware of the gathering darkness.

'I dunno. 'Bout five, I suppose.'

'About five,' she shrieked. 'You there, Tony. C'mon.

We'd better be gettin' home. Mam said to be early tonight, she's going ter take us up ter the club with her and me Dad.'

Tony emerged from the hole they had burrowed into the snow pile. 'Do we have ter? I'd rather stay here.'

'Well, you can't. So get yourself movin'.' Elaine began to propel him along the street.

'Leggo, will yer. I don't want ter go yet. And what about Ma? Aren't we goin' ter go in?'

'Not now, we're not. It's too late fer that.' Peering over the top of her wet and smudgy spectacles, Elaine fixed her brother with a stare that invited no argument.

'Aw, okay. Okay.' Tony trotted obediently along at her side. A few paces further, and they turned with mutual accord to look back towards John standing alone in the darkness.

'Aren't you coming, John?' Tony called.

John hesitated only briefly, then, shrugging his shoulders, he skated along after them.

They had scarcely turned the corner at the end of the street when a meagre shadow detached itself from the surrounding gloom. It passed almost silently over the snow and ice until it stood on the site of the children's recent excavations. Had it been full daylight it is doubtful whether any of the three would have recognized Paul's narrow features in the swollen, distorted face. One eye was lost behind a plum-shaped, prune-coloured swelling, while the other was reduced to a blood-congested slit. His upper lip protruded puffy and broken, making a dreadful parody of the lower half of his face. He moved slowly, one arm held across his chest in a protective attitude. Turning his head from side to side in order to accommodate his restricted vision, he inspected the half-formed snow-tunnel and igloo before making his way around the pile to the entry.

'Stupid little buggers.' He forced the words past his

misshapen lips. 'Got nowt better ter do.' Softly he trod
along the entry and turned into the familiar back yard.
Reaching the lavatory, he groped along the whitewashed
wall to the basin and climbed on the seat to reach the
high metal cistern. He heaved a sigh of relief as his fingers
closed over the key; he'd been half afraid the others would
forget to replace it. All the time he'd been locked in the
bedroom of the flat he had been making plans to get
here, to Ma, as soon as he could. Through the pain and
the misery of his injuries, and the indignity of being locked in
by that big ape his Mam was living with, he had felt a
strange longing to be near the old lady. Somehow, he had
known instinctively that she would give him comfort. Half
sobbing as the cold air caught at the fire in his chest, he
thrust the key home and stepped into the house.

The warmth of the closed sitting-room beat on his
bruised face, setting his blood rushing painfully. A sound
that was part whimper, part groan broke from him. 'Ma.'
The word was barely a whisper, a plea for compassion as
his tortured lips cracked with the effort to pronounce the
name. 'Ma,' he called again, more strongly this time.
Crossing the room, he located the light switch and turned
on the overhead light. The piercing brightness stabbed at
his eye, blinding him in a wash of tears. As they cleared,
Paul turned towards Alice's chair and was astounded at
finding it empty. His head turning from side to side, he
probed every corner of the room. Convinced at last that
he was its only occupant he blundered across the narrow
hall into the dark bedroom. A harsh, rasping noise halted
his footsteps. 'Ma?' he queried, a little nervously. The
rasping continued. Paul held his breath and listened. The
sound came from low down, somewhere near the floor, it
seemed to him. He edged inside the room, his fingers
brushing along the wall, searching for the light switch.

It was cold in here after the heat of the gas fire in the
sitting-room, and a shiver ran down Paul's spine. His

fingers beginning to tremble, he gave up groping at the wall and chanced a step forward towards where he knew the bed to be. The step also brought him nearer the source of the noise, causing the hair to lift on the nape of his neck. On and on it went. Short, sharp, almost a bark.

'Ma.' With an audible gulp Paul forced down his rising fear. 'Answer me, Ma,' he begged of the dark room. With one arm outstretched, the other still held about his chest, he dabbed at the bed. He had fully expected to encounter the warmth of Alice's sleeping form and was disturbed to find only the flat, inanimate covers. 'Ma. Ma, where are you?' He was becoming seriously alarmed now, surely she hadn't given him the slip? Slapping strongly at the bed covers, he worked his way up the bed towards the pillows. If she'd got out, gone to the law, Mick would be certain to kill him. A cold sweat broke out along his skinny body, the memory of that punishing fist too close to be shrugged aside.

'Maaaa.' Paul was becoming frantic now, and his flailing arm caught the bedside lamp, rocking it back against the wall. He grabbed at it and managed to bring it upright. Feeling carefully under the tasselled shade, he located the switch and pressed. The dim light left Alice hidden in the shadows. Paul lifted the lamp, squinting fearfully towards the animal sounds that he found so disturbing. A vague form took shape in the dark shadows under the window. He stared long and hard through the slit of his sighted eye, then replaced the lamp and trod slowly round the bed until he hung over Alice.

As he leaned down, his hand outstretched to pull at her shoulder, the stench of stale urine rose to meet him. He gagged against the acrid fumes and turned his head aside. 'Ma. Ma,' he called imperiously. Why didn't she wake up?

Deeply unconscious, Alice laboured to breathe. Her lungs sawed for air. The fevered grating rose to a crescendo that triggered off a new revulsion in the hovering boy. He was back in the flat, lying beaten and sick on the floor while the panting, gasping, heaving bodies of Mick and his mother writhed and rolled alongside his own.

'Nooooo.' His scream of rage and disgust tore his throat, the split in his lip opened and welled crimson. Hating them. Hating their contact with his flesh, hating their bestial coupling, he kicked out. Savagely, his feet driving like pistons, he kicked. And went on kicking, long after the sound which had driven him to this fury had ceased.

Passion spent, Paul sagged against the bed. The swirling red mist cleared, leaving him shaking with ague. His teeth clattered together and moisture oozed from his inflamed eyes. Both arms wrapped about himself, he rocked to and fro in a shuddering paroxysm. A tide of blood-flecked vomit spewed uncontrollably down his clothing, over the carpet, and across the huddled mound on the floor. Coughing and choking, one arm still bracing his ribs, Paul staggered from the house, leaving the doors swinging open as he blundered through. Outside the house he leaned his shoulders up against the wall and gulped down the clean, fresh-tasting air.

'I didn't mean ter. I didn't mean ter.' He rolled his head against the rough bricks, refuting aloud any responsibility for the horror he'd just committed.

CHAPTER 15

The frosty night air passed like a sponge over the boy's face, steadying him, bringing him to an awareness of the dangers threatening his present situation. He had to get all his stuff cleared away from this place. There would be questions asked when Ma was discovered. He had to make sure the answers didn't lead straight back to him.

It took him several hours to get rid of the magpie hoard in the upstairs room. Some of it he managed to lug across the town and secrete in the vandal-torn garages and store-rooms, originally provided for use of the tenants, under the tower blocks surrounding the one he lived in. Some of it he was forced to smash and tear in his efforts to make it untraceable before he scattered it around the demolished streets. He hated doing it. All the stuff he was breaking up represented money to him, money that would keep him on top and keep the other kids subjected to his will. The destruction of other people's property had never troubled Paul, but this rending and grinding of goods he looked upon as his own awakened his anger.

As he worked, hampered by the near-blindness of his damaged eyes and the stabbing pain in his chest, his anger mounted against Alice. This was all down to her, he raged as he slipped and slithered through the ice bound streets. If she hadn't started pokin' her nose in, and messing things up, none of this lot would have happened. She was just a stupid interfering old cow and she had asked for all she got.

Before passing back into the derelict side of the houses he crossed the back yard and snatched the door of Alice's home closed with a resounding bang. Maybe that 'ud teach her to mind her own bloody business, was his angry reflection. He then turned the key in the lock before flinging it away with an overarm toss that caused him to cry out against the agony it sent coursing through his body.

By the time he'd finished climbing up and down to his former store-room, his fingers, clumsy with cold, were cut and bleeding, adding their share of discomfort to his aching pain-filled misery. Only his feet were divorced from this overall purgatory and they had long ceased to exist, cut off from all feeling by the penetrating cold.

Useless lumps, weighing down his weak rubbery legs, they tripped him at every turn, refusing to follow his desperate attempts to maintain a homeward direction. He didn't want to return to his Mam and that flat, he never wanted to clap eyes on that swine she lived with ever again, but there was no other place for him. He could have stayed with Ma if she hadn't been so bloody stupid. She would have looked after him.

Clawing his way over the snow-hidden rubble, he began cursing Alice anew. Every agonizing fall, every blind plummeting skid, brought fresh invectives from his torn lips. Her fault, her bloody, bloody fault. All her bloody, sodding rotten fault.

Clear of the demolition area, he made better progress across the streets of the town. His feet held and guided by the traffic ruts, he managed to steer a reasonably straight course until he emerged from the network of side roads to enter the cleared apron of concrete giving access to the tower-block flats. Staggering drunkenly now, he reeled into the open, where his unsteady progress caught the attention of the security guard making a perfunctory round of his duties. A big, blustering man, never given to any form of exertion, it was his practice to spend most of the nightly patrol doing his utmost to avoid contact with the intimidating gangs of youths that rampaged the neighbourhood, the very same gangs it was his job to ensure were kept under strict control.

Not for him, though, the role of the hero. He preferred a quieter life and did his best to see that it was so by keeping out of their way. But every now and again he managed to catch one of them alone like this, separated from the rest of the gang for some reason; then he would make the most of the opportunity to throw his weight about and prove his worth to his employers.

At the sight of Paul's diminutive form creeping towards the entrance of the tower blocks, he drew himself up to his full height and stepped boldly forward. Been tipping a bottle somewhere, this one, he thought, noting the unco-ordinated gait. A bloody kid, an' all. Well, he'd just show him this was no place for drunks to come hanging about, school-kid or no.

'What d'yer think yer on with, then?' he demanded loudly, hooking his thumbs into the armpits of his uniform. Then, as Paul stumbled into the circle of light thrown from the flats, the man's bombast fled and his voice dropped on a gasp of shocked disbelief. 'Good God in heaven, lad. Who the hell's done that ter yer?'

Utterly spent, Paul attempted another step forwards, failed, then sagged from the knees, his senseless body toppling brokenly into the outstretched arms of the security guard.

'Sweet Jesus Christ! He's been run over!' The man held Paul's slight form across his arms and gazed around in a helpless fashion. He needed an ambulance, doctors. This kid was in a bad way. Seeing no signs of help forthcoming, he started blindly up the steps to the flats, Paul's arms and legs flapping on each side as his haste increased.

Entering the graffiti-bedecked foyer, he shouldered his way through the broken swing-doors and kicked frantically on the first door he came to. There was no immediate reply, and he passed on down the first-floor landing, kicking each door as he went. At last his efforts were rewarded and one of the doors was flung open as an irate voice bellowed, 'Hey you! What the hell's goin' on here?' after his hurrying figure. By now a frightened panic had rendered the blustering guard almost inarticulate.

'This kid. This kid.' He held Paul's form towards the man, who stood in his shirt-sleeves by the open door.

'What's up wi' 'im?' came the stolid question.

'He's dyin', that's what's up,' screeched the guard.

'Well, he don't belong 'ere.' The man had taken a defensive step backwards into the shelter of his own hallway and he appeared about to pull the door shut.

'Get somebody, you daft bugger. A doctor, man. For Christ's sake.'

'Not me. I'm not gettin' mixed up in no funny business.' The closing door cut off any further comment from the guard.

'You bastard. You stupid, stinking bastard,' he raged at the departed tenant.

'Bring him here.'

About to charge the offending door with his booted feet, the guard barely registered the quiet authoritative tones until they were repeated.

'This way, man. Bring him through. Put him on the couch, I'll ring for an ambulance.'

Thankfully, Paul's befriender carried him along the narrow passageway to the flat's sitting-room, where he laid him gently on the Dralon-covered couch, smearing the pale gold cushions with a mixture of mud and blood. The man who had beckoned them in was already making the telephone call to the emergency services. A woman entered the room from the direction of the kitchen. She carried a hand-towel and was drying her water-reddened hands.

'What's going on, Bert?' she asked of the guard, who was now straightening up from his stooped position over the couch.

'Found him staggering about outside. I think he's a gonner.' The man's face wore a pinched expression as he met her enquiring gaze.

She crossed to the couch and stood for a moment gazing down at Paul's battered face. Hesitantly she stretched out her hand to lay it softly on the boy's forehead. 'He's in a bad way right enough, poor little soul.'

'There's an ambulance on its way.' Her husband dropped the telephone receiver back on its rest and crossed the room to join his wife. 'Let's hope it will get here in time,' he added heavily.

'Oh, Stan, you don't really think . . . ?' Her voice trailed away uncertainly.

'Told yer he was a gonner, didn't I?' Freed of his immediate responsibility towards the injured boy, the security guard regained some of his bravado. 'Knew it the minute as I laid eyes on 'im. Bin hit by a bus. I shouldn't wonder.'

The man exchanged a telling glance with his wife. 'Better get a blanket, love, and cover him up. He looks like he's in shock to me."

The frost hardened overnight and the intense cold of the following day brought traffic chaos on the roads leading into town. Betty Kent tapped impatiently on her steering-wheel as she sat out her second hour in a parade of cars barely crawling along the outer ring-road. A barrage of brake-lights starred against her misted windscreen and she became aware that the slight forward progress was again being halted. Heaving a sigh, she wound down her side window to clear it of condensation and scrubbed at the other windows with a demisting cloth. 'Oh, hell,' she muttered, giving way to the ill humour of enforced inaction. She was tempted to abandon the car and start walking but she thought better of it. It would hardly be fair to leave it stuck on the road in that way, it would only create one more hazard for the rest of the driving population to negotiate. She did get out of the car for a time in an attempt to stamp some life back into her cold legs and feet, but the road surface was glacial and she was afraid she might fall.

Now I know how old folk like Mrs Maxwell must feel, she reflected grimly. Catching hold of the open car door to steady herself, she found her thoughts turning yet again to the old lady and the problem that had been bothering her since she called round on Alice the previous day. Should she follow up her ineffectual visit with any further action, was the question which tormented her as she climbed back into the driving seat. It's not as though she's asked for any help, she reminded herself. And anyway, she might be safe and sound and perfectly well cared for by whichever of her children she has gone to stay with. Wish I could be sure she really *was* staying with one of them, though.

Her brow creased in a worried frown as she stared sightlessly through the windscreen. Why did she have this depressed and wretched feeling that something was wrong? The car in front began to inch forward and Betty gave herself a mental shake as she let in the clutch and crept after it. Can't do anything till I get out of this lot, anyway. She sought refuge from her niggling worry in the obvious truth of this observation and promised herself she'd do something about Alice once she got to the office.

It was nearing midday before Betty had completed her journey and she turned into the office car-park with a gasp of relief.

'Thank the Lord that's over,' she said with feeling, getting out of the car.

'What, you too?' A voice called and she turned to see Marion slithering across the ice towards her. 'I've only just got here myself,' she explained.

'It's a shocker this morning, isn't it? I've been stuck on the ring road since nine o'clock. Nearly three hours.'

'I can't think what's happened to all the grit carts.' Marion complained. 'It's always the same around here. One little fall of snow and the whole county grinds to a halt. It's sickening.'

'Oh, I know. I expect we'll be struggling now until the weather breaks. Still, we can hardly be blamed for being late in; I see Tom Burton's not arrived yet either.' Betty's swift glance around the car-park had noted the absence of her boss's car.

'Don't you believe it. He's lying in wait for us just inside the main office. Must have walked.' Marion pulled a wry face as she and Betty stepped through the outer doors into the reception area. 'He looks like he's seen his backside this morning, so watch out for trouble.'

'Oh, he can knickers,' said Betty with unaccustomed venom. 'I've got enough on my plate without him adding to it.'

Marion raised her eyebrows as she studied her friend. 'What's eating you, then? Can't just be the weather.'

'No it's not,' said Betty shortly. She marched through reception and turned into the ladies' cloakroom, where she flung her bag and the bundle of papers she carried on to the floor under her coat-peg. 'It's this Mrs Maxwell, Marion,' she said, and turned in the act of removing her coat, the better to see her companion's reaction. 'I can't seem to get her out of my mind just lately. She's been haunting me for days now. What do you think I should do?'

Marion studied the worried face for a moment or two before making any reply. She knew from experience that the nature of their work sometimes meant an involvement that was too close to permit a balanced view. It was best not to become too concerned with people as individuals. Much better to treat each case as a problem to be solved and dealt with along prescribed lines without ever digging into the human factor involved. Otherwise these things could push a perfectly good officer into making all sorts of rash decisions.

'I wasn't aware there was any problem, or even that we were involved,' she said, still watching Betty's face.

'Well, there is and there isn't.' Betty fiddled with her gloves, trying to analyze her feelings about this case and discuss it with sensible detachment. 'I went round there yesterday and . . .' Her voice trailed away as she failed to find the words she needed.

'And?' Marion prompted as the silence wore on.

'And she wasn't there . . . I couldn't get into the house . . . And . . . And I know she can't walk out, not in this sort of weather.' Betty finished her feeble explanation in an embarrassed rush.

'Papers in the letter-box? Milk on the doorstep?' Marion enquired coolly.

'No. Nothing like that. It's just that . . . that . . .'

'Just that you've got a feeling.'

'Well, yes. I suppose that's all it is really.'

'Hmmmm, you know, Betty, it's easy when you're fairly new to this game to get a bit carried away. I've seen it happen before.'

'Yes, but . . .' Betty tried to cut in, only to have Marion continue, 'When you've been here as long as I have you'll learn more sense. In the meantime—' she gave an understanding smile—'we'll see what we can fish out of the files about your Mrs Maxwell,' she concluded.

'Oh, Marion, thanks. I'd feel a lot better.' Betty returned the smile, her spirits lifting.

'Yes, well, tell me if you still feel better after we've heard what Tom Burton's got to say. Come on.'

Tom Burton was the area supervisor and could usually be relied upon to give his staff a fair hearing, but his problems had begun more than two hours ago when he'd abandoned his car and walked into work only to find himself the only officer present when all the telephones shrilled into life. It hadn't helped when the social worker from the children's hospital, herself on the receiving end of some very tricky questions, had begun making pointed enquiries about a case he had long since thought to have heard the last about.

'What do you know about a Paul Raymond Collins?' he snapped towards the two girls as they entered the office. 'Come on, come on. Don't stand about gawping now you've finally deigned to turn up. I want some answers and I want them like yesterday. There's a case about to go badly wrong just now and I'm getting sick of being the one to carry the can.'

'Paul Collins?' Marion was the first to volunteer. 'What address?'

'The tower blocks, where else?' Tom rifled bad temperedly through a stack of folders he'd lifted from the filing cabinet.

'Pennine House? Is that the one?' Marion experienced a twinge of concern. That particular case had once been in her charge.

'That's the one. Have you got it?' Tom turned eagerly.

'I . . . er . . . I think it's in the dead file,' she offered hesitantly.

'Christ! It would be.' Tom scrubbed distractedly at his receding hairline. 'There's a right hoo-haa going on over at the children's hospital. Better get the thing out and bring it into my office.'

'Right away,' promised Marion, moving towards the row of metal filing cabinets.

'What's it all about, do you think?' Betty whispered watching the door swing to behind their boss.

'Lord knows. But you can bet it's not going to cover us with roses,' Marion said drily, yanking a well-thumbed file out of a drawer.

'Hmm, this is the case all right.' She muttered vaguely as she skimmed quickly through the contents of the file. 'Bit old for the Children's, I would have thought. Thirteen. Thirteen and a half, to be exact. Still . . .'

'What sort of a case is it, Marion? Should we have been keeping an eye on it?' Betty asked anxiously, feeling immediate responsibility for any implied negligence.

'No, no . . . At least . . . Well, no. I don't really think so. It was thoroughly investigated before we decided to close our files.' She glanced at Betty. 'Oh, don't look so flaming guilty, girl. It's hardly your fault in any event.' Her own misgivings made her short with the younger girl, and she was instantly contrite. 'Sorry, Betty. I shouldn't take it out on you, I know. Look, why don't you go and make us all a coffee? I'm sure I could murder a cup.'

'Okay.' Betty smiled to show she harboured no resentment. 'If you are quite sure there is nothing else I can do?' she offered as she crossed obediently to the cupboard where they kept their supplies of tea and coffee.

'No, I've told you. Go on. Scoot.' Marion shooed her out and burrowed deeper into the Collins file, a frown growing between her gently arched brows. There were times when this job could be sheer hell, she thought as she read. One needed to be clairvoyant, on top of all else, to see it through properly. So deep was her concentration that she accepted the proffered cup of coffee from her friend without even noticing. Oh Lord. There was so much, and yet so little, to be read into this case. Stuffing the papers back into the folder, she marched resignedly towards her boss's office.

Tom Burton had recovered sufficient of his good humour by the time Marion placed the file on his desk to offer her an apology.

'Thanks, Marion. Sorry I yelled at you just now, but all hell's been let loose in here this morning.'

'That's okay. Where is everybody, anyway?'

'You may well ask. Greg phoned in to say he couldn't make it. Arthur and Bill are working from home since they'll have to go on foot, thanks to the weather. Jenny is off with the flu, and Brenda is on two days' leave.'

'Never rains, does it?' Marion sympathized. 'Well, what's with the Collins boy?'

'Someone has beaten him up, seems to be the mother.' Tom flicked through the bulky file. 'You know, this case should never have been closed. Just look at all this bumph. Truancy, theft, broken home, etc., etc., etc. He's perfect material for our department.'

'But there's no real history of cruelty, is there?' Marion

was so surprised at her boss's opening sentence she missed most of the rest of his speech. 'How bad is it?'

'Pretty bad. Bloody awful, in fact. Black eyes, broken ribs, multiple contusions, and now he's delirious. Keeps rambling on about his Ma. Says she did it. All her fault, he's told the hospital doctors. They don't know yet if he'll pull through, seems one of the ribs pierced his lung.'

'Poor little devil,' said Marion with heartfelt concern. 'I never get used to these child-bashings, you know.' She paused reflectively, trying to recall what she knew of the case. 'I don't remember any suspicions of this sort concerning his mother before, though,' she was forced to admit.

'No.' Tom heaved a sigh. 'But you know how it is. They cover things up so cleverly these days, and it's quicker to lash out at the kids to keep them quiet than it is to get up and turn the telly off while they listen to what they have to say.'

Marion murmured agreement.

'Better leave this with me now, Marion. I'll get back to the hospital and see what action they want.'

'Probably your head on a plate,' Marion told him as she left his office, 'or mine,' she added under her breath.

'Grim, was it?' Betty asked, noting her gloomy expression when she returned to the general office.

'And likely to get worse.'

'Oh, no. Not another of those, "And what were the Social Workers doing?" ' Betty spoke in a derisive falsetto.

' 'Fraid so. A child-bashing of the worst sort. But you needn't upset yourself. It's an old case, before your time.' Marion did her best to appear optimistically cheerful.

'Yes, but still . . .' Betty offered her sympathy in a lift of her shoulders.

'I've told you, it's not your worry,' said Marion firmly, and returned to her desk to make a show of beginning some paperwork. 'But he was such a little scrap of a boy, if I remember it right,' she said, giving up all pretence and gazing off into space. 'I mean, what could that child possibily have done to warrant anyone, least of all his own mother, beating him so?'

Betty sent her a glance of commiseration. 'I know how you must feel, Marion. But try to remember what you always tell me; don't let yourself get too involved.'

'It's just the kids though, Bett. I can't help it. They are always the ones to suffer, poor helpless, hopeless little beggars.' The two exchanged expressive nods, and as if by common consent allowed the subject to drop while they busied themselves with the files on their desks.

The pending row over the Paul Collins case, the acute staff shortage and the problem of getting through her day's workload within the limits of the time left to her, drove all thought of the crippled old lady out on Princess Street from Betty's mind. It wasn't until she plodded back to the office well after her usual finishing time that she again remembered her half-formed intention to pay her a visit. She hovered over the filing cabinets, too cold, wet and tired to make the simple decision of whether to look into the case that night or leave it over until the morning. The clank made by the cleaning woman's bucket as she slopped it inside the office door settled the matter for her. She was too spent to cope with any problems that would have to be dealt with while someone mopped the floor around her feet. She would just have to look into the Mrs Maxwell business tomorrow. Collecting up her bag and gloves, she rubbed the back of her neck wearily before heading towards the cloakroom.

If Alice had nagged at Betty Kent's conscience over the course of the week, she had been no less in the mind of her taxi-driver friend. On this Thursday morning he nursed his cab over the perilous roads to Alice's door knowing she would rely on him to call for her as usual in spite of the snow and ice. I don't know why one of those kids she does so much for can't help her out a bit in weather like this, he thought critically. It wouldn't kill one of them to run a few errands for her. Reaching the house, he applied the hand-brake and gave his pip-pip tattoo as he climbed out of the cab. There was no answering salute from the window and he continued to watch for the giveaway twitch of the curtains as he passed round the back of the taxi to reach the pavement. ' 'Sfunny.' His brows drew together. 'Come on, Mrs M, show a leg,' he called as he reached the front door. He gave a couple of knocks and waited before turning back to peer through the window.

'Taxi, Mrs M.' His breath fogged the glass and he rubbed away the misted patch to get a better view. The room appeared to be empty. Puzzled, and getting a little worried now, he took a step back to survey the front of the house. Mrs M was never late. She was always waiting, ready to open the door the minute his cab drew to a halt. It was then he noticed the bottles of milk awaiting collection on the snow-covered windowsill. Never, in all the time he'd been running Alice into town, had he known her leave the milk out until this time of day. 'Oh, God.' Thoroughly alarmed he strode rapidly down the entry and across the back yard.

'Mrs Maxwell. Are you all right?' He banged heavily on the back door. 'Mrs Maxwell, it's me, Ron.'

He tried the door and pushed against it in vain. The gas fire continued to burn, lending a cheerful light to the slice of room he could see through the window. But a cold hand clutched at his stomach. Something was wrong. He could feel it.

'Mrs Maxwell,' he called once again in hopeless desperation. He was no longer expecting to get a reply. Now he didn't know what to do for the best; the door refused to yield to his kicks and thuds, yet he continued to beat against it until he was breathless. Now, think, man.

Think! He ordered himself to refrain from the crazy attack on the door and made a deliberate return to common sense. She could be perfectly all right, maybe out somewhere. No. He rejected the thought as too bloody daft to be laughed at. There was no way she could go out in this lot. He glanced round at the piled snow for confirmation. Then perhaps she had been taken ill, and one of the kids had fetched somebody to see she was taken care of. Nah, he didn't really go for that explanation either. All takers and no givers, them kids, if he knew anything. Then what?

Well, he wasn't going to stand here guessing any longer. Taking off his shoe, he hefted it until he held it by the toe, then, using the heel as a hammer, he smashed the window glass around the old-fashioned central catch. Slipping his hand through the jagged hole, he released the catch and was able to slide the bottom frame up on the sash cords. Taking a deep breath against the plunging dread he was feeling, he steeled himself to climb in through the window. Now that he'd come this far he was reluctant to go on. There was an eerie feeling about the old house. In spite of the steady hiss from the gas fire, Ron was aware of a deep, eternal silence.

'Are you there, Mrs Maxwell?' he called, trying to give himself the courage to start across the room to the far door which he knew must lead to the bedroom.

'Hello?' The silence ate into him.

With a sudden squaring of his shoulders he strode across the room, made no pause in the small hallway, but went on through to the bedroom.

CHAPTER 16

He didn't see Alice at first.

His anxious gaze had gone straight to the bed, and his relief at finding it empty expelled the air from his lungs in a juddering gasp. Before his whispered 'Thank God' had faded from his hearing, his eyes were caught and held by the glint of light playing along the shiny metal of Alice's walking-frame. He allowed his gaze to travel reluctantly along the fallen rods until they became lost to sight behind the hanging bedcovers.

Slowly, he stepped around the end of the bed.

It might have been a bundle of rags tossed in the careless heap under the window. It might have been, only rags don't bleed. And these had. In a wide sticky pool that matted the loose fabric of her clothing to the worn stubby pile of the carpet.

Ron swallowed painfully. He didn't need to touch the outstretched hand, nor examine closer the sick gleam of white bone that had pierced the clothing over the shattered ribcage, to know that a savage, pitiless death had walked in this room.

He clutched convulsively at the edge of the dressing-table, the hard wood cutting into the palm of his hand.

'Dear God in heaven.' Hanging over her body, unable to move in his horror, he fought to tear his eyes away from the sight.

'Oh, Christ Almighty. NO!' With a wild cry he flung himself around and staggered back into the sitting-room. In there, he leaned his outstretched arms on the table's edge and let his spinning head sag forwards between his arms while the stinging salt tears washed the taste of bile from his mouth.

He gulped raggedly for air, choked, and gagged on his indrawn breath.

At last he straightened and scrubbed at his face with the palm of his hand. He'd better go for the police, he supposed.

The back door had a mortice lock, and there was no key in evidence. Ron gave a cursory glance round the small kitchen but was unable to locate it, so he turned about and left the house through the window which had given him entry. Driving far too fast for the prevailing conditions, he slewed his taxi across the end of the street and wrenched it into a skidding halt on the wrong side of the road as he caught sight of the uniformed constable heading for duty on some school crossing.

The blanched green-white face staring through the windscreen warned the policeman that this was no ordinary case of reckless driving.

'It's murder. There's been a murder. Get in, man, get in. I'll take you.' Ron was past coherent thought or common politeness. He reached for the rear doorhandle and pushed the door wide.

'Just a minute, sir. I'll travel up front, if you don't mind.' Eyeing his man with a speculative stare, the policeman closed the door and paced round the rear of the cab before slipping into the front passenger seat. 'Now hold on, hold on,' he cautioned as Ron appeared about to continue his wild, erratic course. 'Just tell me a little about it before we start off.'

Ron gulped air, the constable's calm manner helping to steady his tormented nerves. 'It's the old lady. I . . . I . . . take her out every week . . . Thursdays . . . Pension day, you know.' He beat his fist against the steering-wheel in blind frustration as he struggled to marshall his thoughts. There was a pain deep under his ribs; it would be with him a long time, he thought. He had let her down. Betrayed her, at a time when she needed him most. Why in God's name hadn't he called round the other day when the thought of her, here, alone, had crossed his mind?

The heavy silence of the old house seemed to enter the cab, pressing in on its occupants. Ron bowed his head under the weight of its accusation. So old. She had been so old, so frail, and so alone. What a way to end eighty years of life. Surely she had deserved better than that.

Seconds ticked away. The constable, staring straight ahead, seemed to sense some of Ron's bitter self-recrimination.

'It was hardly your fault, sir,' he said suddenly, as if in reply to some outburst.

Ron made no answer.

'Shall we be on our way, then?' The uniformed arm lifted, indicating the road ahead.

Ron didn't see the gesture, his eyes were not perceiving their immediate surroundings.

The constable coughed politely, hoping to draw his attention, and failed in the attempt. 'This won't do, you know, sir.' He was obliged to jolt Ron back to the business in hand by reaching over to take a grip on the steering-wheel.

'They want topping, the swines.' Ron ground the words through clenched teeth, a hint of hysteria edging his voice.

'I'm sure you are right, sir,' came the placating reply, giving Ron time to regain a little of his composure. The threatened hysterics subsided, to be supplanted by a righteous anger.

'I knew there was something. I just knew.' He spat the words almost savagely.

'Suppose you tell me your name, sir.' Again the calm, steady voice holding him in check.

'Ron . . . I . . . I . . . Oh, sorry, officer. You must think I'm a bloody nut.' Ron tried again. 'I'm Ronald

Sheldrick. This is my own cab. I have a standing arrangement to pick up . . . to pick up . . .'

The constable, studying the set face, saw the nerve jump along the tense jawline, twitching the blood-drained lips into a grimace, and gave up his attempt to draw the man further.

'Let's just make our way there, nice and steady like, shall we, Mr Sheldrick?'

'Huh? Oh, yes. Yes, sorry.' Ron eased in the clutch and the cab moved forward. He was staring straight ahead. At the packed ice and snow crunching in protest under his wheels. But he was seeing again the inside of an old lady's bedroom.

The taxi turned into the narrow street, tilting badly as always on the steep camber. The constable looked about him, taking note of the demolition in progress and the almost desolate air of the remaining dwelling. Ron drew the cab to a halt, its bonnet nudging the piled snow fallen from the roof.

'In there . . . I . . . She . . .' Ron shook his head, his voice failing him.

The constable shot him a swift glance, made as if to speak, then kept his silence as he pushed open the cab door.

'Just you wait here, sir. I'll be back in a jiffy,' he said as he stepped out onto the pavement. He ploughed over the ice-rutted snow, pausing only briefly at the front window. Passing the door, he tried the handle, then gave up and disappeared into the maw of the entry.

When he re-appeared his face wore a greyish sheen and he was breathing heavily as he dropped into the passenger seat. Neither man spoke.

'You'll need to get help, I suppose.' Ron was beginning to come out of the first numbing effects of shock.

'I'll radio in. Best if we stay here, keep an eye on the place till the boss arrives.' He pushed open the cab door and climbed out onto the pavement, taking his radio from a clip on his belt.

Ron listened to the metallic jabber from the instrument without making any sense of the words. A heavy sense of guilt was fastening upon him. He should have looked in on the old lady. He knew she wasn't fit to be left alone. Wouldn't have killed him, just to keep an eye on her. Now she was gone—slain—massacred. The vision he knew was to haunt him the rest of his life painted itself on his windscreen, and he dropped his head between his hands clenched on the steering-wheel.

The constable climbed back into the taxi. 'Shouldn't be long now, sir. Nasty business. Must have given you quite a turn, finding her like that.' His professionalism came to the fore, putting the trite words into the prescribed placating formula.

Ron let them pass without comment. He was lost in thoughts of revenge. He'd like to get his hands on the swine responsible, he'd give him what for. His knuckles whitened as his grip tightened on the wheel.

A long blue car turned into the street. 'Ah, this looks like them. Will you just wait a little longer, sir, shan't keep you hanging about now. We'll need to go down to the station and get your statement, then you can be on your way.' The taxi door opened.

'Statement?' Ron stared up at the metal buttons fronting the constable's tunic.

'That's right, sir. We'll need all the details, I'm afraid.'

'I see,' said Ron quietly. I see too bloody much, his thoughts accused him. I see all the times I've passed by this way these last few days and never bothered to look in.

The occupants of the blue car stood in conversation with the constable for a while, then they all disappeared towards the rear of the house. They were still inside when Betty Kent's bright red Mini pulled to a halt opposite. She scrambled out, finding it difficult to keep her footing on the old street. There was a worried expression on her face as she crossed to Ron's taxi.

'Excuse me.' She rapped on his side window, breaking in on his angry thoughts. 'I'm sorry to bother you,' she said as he pushed the door open, 'but do you happen to know what's going on?'

'Why? Come to rubber-neck, have you?' Ron said nastily, not caring who he hurt in his need to lash out.

'No . . . I . . . I'm sorry. I shouldn't have troubled you.' Betty drew back hastily. Her sudden movement jerked her feet from beneath her and she fell sprawling against the rear of the taxi.

Ron was instantly contrite and hurried from the cab to lift her to her feet. 'Sorry. I shouldn't have said that. Are you all right?'

'Yes, I think so. But what *is* going on? Is there something wrong at Mrs Maxwell's?'

Ron stiffened. 'Were you coming to see her?' he asked carefully.

'Well, yes. You see, I'm a Welfare Officer, and —'

'And making a bloody mess of the job, same as all the rest,' Ron flung at her.

'Now, just you look here —' Betty's temper rose at this second attack from this man who was a complete stranger to her.

But he gave her no chance to continue.

'No. You look here, Miss. Mrs Maxwell is dead. D'yer hear me? Dead. And if you'd been doing your job as you ought . . . Oh, what's the use.' Ron turned away, the anger going from him as he realized the futility of it all.

'Dead? Oh, no.' Stunned, Betty stared at Ron's averted head. 'When?' she asked, dreading his reply. When he made no answer she asked again. 'When did it happen? Not . . . Not yesterday, was it?'

Ron turned slowly. 'Why not yesterday? Do you know something? See somebody?'

'No, I . . . Well, if you must know, it's just that I'd made up my mind to come and see her yesterday, only . . . only . . .'

'Yeah. Only you didn't make it. I know just how you feel.' Ron paused, reflecting the truth of his words. 'Well, I don't know when it was, except there are two bottles of milk on the sill, so I should think it was before yesterday.'

'But I was here on Tuesday,' Betty said slowly. 'She didn't answer the door and I looked through the windows, back and front. The house appeared to be empty.'

'You were here?' Ron looked at her keenly. 'Look, the police are inside, I think you'd better wait and see them.'

'The police?' Betty looked bewildered. 'But why?'

'Why the police, or why is she lying in there with her chest stoved in?' Ron was unable to resist the bitter question, the pathetically broken body still clear in his mind.

Betty stared at him, too sick to speak, her hand went out groping for support against the side of the taxi.

Ron was jolted out of his painful preoccupation. 'Look here, love. Are you all right? I'm sorry about all this, but I found her, you see. Just a bit ago.'

'I see . . . Yes, I should have guessed.' Betty recovered her voice, realizing for the first time some of the strain Ron was under. 'No wonder you . . . Well, never mind that now. It's my turn to say sorry, you must think me completely heartless.'

'No, you couldn't have known.' Ron brushed aside her apology.

'You said . . . You said she had her chest . . . Had she been attacked?'

'She has been murdered,' said Ron flatly. 'Smashed.' He swallowed convulsively before adding, 'I just hope they catch the bastard that did it, that's all.'

'Have they any idea?'

'Shouldn't think so, not yet. They've only just got here.' They fell silent, each busy with their own thoughts.

'What about her family? Have they been told?' Betty ventured at last.

'Family? What family?' Ron stared at her, surprised.

'Well, when I called a week or so back she said something about children. I assumed she meant her own children — her family.'

'Her only son lives abroad, Australia, I think. There's nobody else.'

'But I'll swear she said the children came to see her most days. Are you sure . . . I mean . . . if it hadn't been for that . . .' Her voice trailed away. What use now to insist that she would have made certain the old lady had some sort of supervision, had she but known.

'She must have meant the kids. I'd forgotten about them. They're no relations, mind. Just a handful of kids that live somewhere hereabouts. Mrs M used to make quite a fuss of them.'

Before Betty could make any further comment the constable reappeared. 'Nothing more you and I can do here, sir,' he said to Ron before turning to Betty. 'Morning, Miss.' His voice held a note of enquiry, and Betty rushed in to explain her business.

'Hmmm, Welfare Officer, did you say?' The constable scribbled in a small notebook. 'Just give me your name and your phone number at the department. We'll be in touch later, I expect.'

Taking the constable's tone as one of dismissal, Betty hurried to excuse herself and returned to her car.

'I think we can be getting along to the station now, sir. No sense in hanging about here.' The policeman was firmly insistant.

'Just a minute, constable. There is something.' Ron paused wondering how to phrase his request. 'There are some kids, they come around most days to see the old lady.' He jerked his head to indicate the house. 'I was wondering . . . she was very fond of them . . . I wouldn't like them to find out by walking in on all this. Do you think we could let them know in some way?' He looked at the constable expectantly and met a narrowed gaze.

'Kids. What sort of kids? Little kids? Big kids? Rowdy kids? Yobbos?' The questions were shot at him.

'Oh, no. No, nothing like that,' Ron hastened to assure him. 'Just two or three little kids. There was one bigger lad, but . . .' He fell silent. Should he voice his opinion of the type of kids he'd seen hanging around here? They'd never seemed particularly lovable to him . . . but all the same . . . No. Better not. Mrs M had been very fond of them, it wouldn't be fair of him to pull them to pieces now that she was gone.

'But? But what, sir?' The constable prodded Ron's wandering thoughts back into line.

'Eh? Oh. But he was a bit backward like — seemed quiet enough, though.' said Ron hastily.

'Any idea where they all live?'

'Not really. I had a vague impression that one of them lived over in the new tower blocks . . . something Mrs Maxwell once said . . .'

'Can't give me his name, I suppose? I mean, those tower blocks.' The constable pulled a wry face.

Ron lowered his chin to his chest, his face creased with the effort of concentration. 'Paul. Paaaul . . . er . . . Collins, I think.'

'Paul Collins.' The constable applied his pen to his leather-bound note book. 'And the others, sir? Any ideas?'

' 'Fraid not. They called the big dopey lad Ginger. But then they would, wouldn't they? Him having hair like the setting sun.' Ron lapsed into an avenue of thought which the other man made no effort to penetrate. His patience was presently rewarded. 'And the fat girl was one of 'em's sister. I remember now. Two fair-haired kids, boy and girl. The girl was fat, like I said, with glasses. . . Then there was another boy. Small, brown hair. Young John, Mrs Maxwell called him. John.' He turned to the police- man in some disappointment. 'Not much help that, is it?'

'You'd be surprised, sir. You'd be surprised.' He tucked the notebook back into his tunic pocket. 'Quite a little band, that. Must have been somebody noticed them if they regularly went about together. We'll put the wheels in motion back at the station, don't you worry. We'll soon know who they are.'

'Well, it's just that I'd hate them to . . . to . . .' Ron cast an agonized glance at the house and the constable was quick to forestall any further break in his companion's newly-won composure.

'Let's get along now, sir. If you please,' he requested quietly. And, folding his arms across his chest, he leant back in his seat with every expectation of being obliged.

There was no way either Ron or the constable could have anticipated the electric reaction that the name of Paul Collins produced.

'That's the second time I've heard his name in as many hours,' The desk sergeant exclaimed, rising excitement robbing him of the caution he normally displayed when it came to disclosing police business before a member of the public. 'There's an incident report in. He's been badly beaten up. Here, George!' He turned to an officer seated by a complex switchboard. 'Better give upstairs a buzz, they'll be wanting to hear this.' He turned back to Ron and the constable. 'Take him straight up, Chris,' he ordered, nodding his head towards a partly opened door as Ron and his companion exchanged startled glances.

'This way, Mr Sheldrick. It's to be hoped we can find those children of yours before they are very much older.' The uniformed figure started briskly in the direction in- dicated, closely followed by the taxi-driver.

In spite of the constable's earnest desire, it was after

seven that evening when Policewoman Boxall pulled the patrol car into the off-loading bay alongside Pennine House. She waited for the CID sergeant to climb out of the front passenger seat before she slid from the steamy warm confines into the biting cold wind that tugged at the skirt of her heavy topcoat.

'Brrr, it's enough to freeze the ball . . . Oh, . . . um . . . Jeez, it's arctic tonight, don't you think?' The detective-sergeant was new to the division.

Sue Boxall risked a conspiratorial grin. 'Shouldn't think there'd be many brass monkeys about, myself,' she said as they passed through the vandalized entrance doors.

The institutional smell, comprising stale urine, boiled cabbage and unwashed human feet, hung like a pall in the air. Sue thumbed the lift button hopefully. 'You never know. It might still be working,' she said, glancing up at the illuminated panel set high in the wall. 'Ah.' A sharp 'ping' announced the arrival of the narrow box behind the reeded steel guarding the lift shaft. The doors rumbled apart. Sue and the sergeant stepped into the lift to stare blankly at the long row of buttons indicating the floors.

'Which?' The sergeant, hand upraised, placed the onus on the young policewoman.

'About twenty-two, I should think.'

'Twenty-two it is, then.'

They travelled upwards in silence and had stepped into the communal hallway of the twenty-second floor before a glance at the nearest door confirmed they were a couple of flights short.

'Come on. We'll hike the rest.' Sue climbed gamely after the sergeant, the bare concrete steps ringing under the tread of their feet. On the twenty-fourth floor they arrived at the door they were seeking.

Paul's mother answered their knock. She was newly

made up and dressed for an evening out at the local; the smell of hair lacquer was sucked out into the landing as she pulled back the door.

'Mrs Collins?' Sue gasped as she made the enquiry. The climb up the stairs had shortened her breath, and the perfumed lacquer caught at her throat.

'That's right. Can I help you?' Jenny Collins, her voice schooled into genteel tones, peered between heavily mascara'd lashes from one to the other.

'Is it about Paul?' she asked quickly, one hand fluttering up over her cleavage to clutch dramatically at the base of her throat. 'Is he . . . He's not . . .?'

'There's no change in his condition as far as we know, Mrs Collins,' Sue assured her, a grim note creeping into her voice as she added, 'for which you may count yourself lucky.'

'Lucky . . . Me . . . ?' Jenny stared at the policewoman, completely missing the point. '*I've* never had much luck, I can tell you that.'

'Then perhaps you would like to invite us in and tell us a little bit more.' Sue pushed against the door. 'We are here to listen, the sergeant and I — Policewoman Boxall — Detective-Sergeant Stone.' She effected the introduction without easing the pressure against the door, and Jenny stepped back, sensing a certain purpose in the girl's manner.

She led the way into the untidy sitting-room and waved them towards the settee. 'S-sit down . . . Please.'

'We'll stand, thanks.' Stone answered for them both. 'Now, Mrs Collins. About your son?' He raised quizzical eyebrows. 'Care to tell us how he came by those appalling injuries?'

Jenny shot nervous glances from his face to the policewoman's. 'I . . . I. No. I . . . No idea.'

'Get a bit too much for you, did he? Felt you'd had enough? Was that it?'

'No . . . No, not me . . . I.'

'Then who, Mrs Collins? . . . If not you, who else does he call Ma?' Stone's voice was rippling silk.

Jenny bit at the thick lipstick coating her lower lip, and Sue Boxall, interpreting a signal from Stone, stepped forward to take her by the arm and lead her to a chair.

'Might as well tell us, love,' she invited quietly. 'Save yourself a whole lot of bother.'

'But I didn't . . . I didn't.' Jenny shook her head vigorously, trying by the force of her denial to convince them.

'Then why should he say it was you?' Sue questioned steadily.

'He *can't* have . . . He can't, he knows I never.'

'His Ma. He told the doctors. Ma. Didn't you hear?' The voice was low and friendly, betraying no note of accusation.

'But he never calls me Ma . . . Only Mam, always Mam . . . That shows you, doesn't it?' Jenny's face was alight with triumph. Maybe *now* they'd believe her. She got up from her chair in a fever to have them leave before Mick made an appearance.

'Just a minute, Mrs Collins. That's not good enough, I'm afraid. The state your son is in it's very difficult to be precise about his actual words. His mouth is very swollen, as you are no doubt aware.' Sue's voice hardened in spite of herself. 'He could easily have meant, or even said, Mam.'

'No. You're wrong . . . He . . .' Jenny's protests died away as Mick came into the room.

'What's up, Jen? What's going on?' Mick was stripped to the waist, and a damp face-towel spread between his hands bore evidence of his having just come from the bathroom.

'It's the perlice, Mick. They think it was me as hit our Paulie.' Jenny forgot her careful accent in her rush to in-

form Mick of the situation and prevent any possibly in-
discreet comment from him.

'Then you must be daft,' Mick informed them bluntly.
'She's never laid a finger on him, not all the time I've bin
here. Too bloody soft, if you ask me.'

'I take it you are not the boy's father.' Stone eyed Mick's
heavy girth speculatively.

'No, I'm not. And I'm thankful fer that,' Mick stated.

'Then . . . ?'

'I'm a friend. A friend of the family, yer might say. I
look in from time to time. Help out a bit, like.' Mick
began to hedge, remembering the ignominy of his last
flight from this place.

'Bit of a tearaway, is he? The lad?' Stone's voice was full
of fraternal understanding.

'Tearaway! Not bloody much. He's hell on two wheels
when he gets goin'. *She* can't handle him. Comin' in here
with his pockets stuffed full of fags. He . . .' Mick
stopped. In his bid to secure a sympathetic hearing he
had already said too much.

'Oh, Mick. What d'yer want ter go and tell them that
for? Now you've got ter tell them the rest.' Jenny Collins's
face had crumpled into a painted mask of reproach and
despair.

'He's a bloody little thief. That's what he is — what they
all are — Well, I'll tell you straight. I've pasted him!
Pasted him good and proper. He'll think twice afore he
does it again. And if them others was ter get theirs,
there'd be no need for the likes of your poxy lot.' Mick was
yelling now, guilt and fear prodding him into a self-
righteous rage.

Policewoman and sergeant exchanged a long glance.
When Mick's tirade was spent, Sue Boxall was waiting,
notebook in hand.

'*You* hit him?'

'Yes, I bloody well hit him. That's what I said, ain't it?'

'Better give me your full name, please.'

'Shaunessy. Michael James Shaunessy,' came the sullen reply.

'Then I must warn you, Michael James Shaunessy, that you are not obliged to say . . .'

'And I must warn you, Miss high and bloody mighty, that I'm not in this by me todd. No, by God! There's others in this. And I only hope as how you'll hound them same as how you'll hound me.' Anger rose again in a swift crimson tide across Mick's contorted features. 'They might only be sweet innocent kids ter your lot. But I know better. I know what cunnin' little bastards they really are.'

'Names and addresses, Shaunessy. Just names and addresses.' Stone's voice was crisp.

'I'll give yer names and addresses. I'll give yer the whole soddin' lot.'

'You can cut out the trimmings, Shaunessy. Just give us the facts.'

'Facts! What would your lot know about facts, if it wasn't fer the likes of me? Only here to be pushed around, I am, aren't I? Like muck under a brush. Well, before you start pushin', just get a snootful of this.' His lungs were empty of air, but he was far too pent up to pause. His voice rasped in his throat as he raged on. 'Them there kids are all practising thieves. They go around the town pinchin' stuff — not your twopenny-ha'penny rubbish, neither — good stuff. Expensive stuff. Radios and such. They've even got a bloody fence workin' for them.' Mick halted his tirade and took a deep gulp of air. He was beginning to enjoy this. The expression on Policewoman Boxall's face told him his disclosures were all news in that direction at least.

Picking his words for effect now, he told them: 'They operate like an organized mob. Stealin', storin', sellin'. Everything planned. Everything thought of. Got some poor old bugger so flummoxed with their comin's and goin's, shouldn't think she knows if she's on this earth or Fuller's.'

'*What*? What's that about some old b—old woman?' Stone jumped in so quickly he stumbled over Mick's choice of words.

Now it was Mick's turn to stare. The old woman's part in all this had seemed secondary to him. He had mentioned her only to spin out his story and give that po-faced young bitch a bit more scribbling to do.

'Come on, man,' Stone ordered, 'I'm waiting for the details.'

'I er, they . . .'

'Come on. Come on.' Stone began to drum his fingers against the back of the chair recently vacated by Jenny.

'She's some old girl round in the clearance area. They use her place ter store their loot, so ter speak.'

'Name of?' Stone knew the name before it was spoken, as did Policewoman Boxall.

Their eyes met and held, a sickness growing out of their silence.

'Maxwell,' Mick ventured.

'Maxwell,' Stone echoed softly. 'Yes.' He nodded his head without knowing he did so, the slow, thoughtful motion spelling out his reading of the situation.

'Better give me all the names you've got, Shaunessy,' he said. So deep was his sigh, it robbed Mick of his last ounce of bluster. And he began with a queer sense of sorrow to intone the list that only a few minutes before he would have spouted with relish.